Peter Cooper

The Political and Financial Opinions of Peter Cooper

With an autobiography of his early life

Peter Cooper

The Political and Financial Opinions of Peter Cooper
With an autobiography of his early life

ISBN/EAN: 9783337113827

Printed in Europe, USA, Canada, Australia, Japan

Cover: Foto ©Raphael Reischuk / pixelio.de

More available books at **www.hansebooks.com**

FINANCIAL OPINIONS

OF

PETER COOPER.

WITH AN

AUTOBIOGRAPHY OF HIS EARLY LIFE.

EDITED BY

Prof. J. C. ZACHOS,

CURATOR AT THE COOPER UNION.

New York.

———

New York:

TROW'S PRINTING AND BOOKBINDING COMPANY,

205–213 East Twelfth Street.

1877.

PREFACE.

The "opinions," financial and political, formed by Mr. Peter Cooper and given in the following pages, have been the result of much anxious thought, reading, and reflection during the last five years, under the pressure laid on every thoughtful mind and patriotic heart by the current events of the times. These events, confessedly, both in politics and in finance, have been disastrous and unhappy upon the interests and prosperity of the American people. Men have been divided as to the true reasons of this unhappy state of facts, but still all are agreed that such facts exist, and the causes of our political and financial troubles should be dispassionately inquired into, and the remedies should be applied speedily; for we are fast drifting, as a nation, into anarchy and ruin. *The republic is in danger*, and it behooves every man to be at his post as a citizen and a *voter*. The questions involved are very simple, and with a little reflection and true patriotism, the simple ideas involved in the public policy of this government can be understood by every intelligent voter.

Methods of *administration* are sometimes very difficult to determine, and require large experience and great knowledge of affairs. But the *principles* of public policy on which parties are formed, are generally very simple, and can be understood by the average American mind, if men would but use their own reason, and not pin their faith to party leaders whose interest it may be to mislead the people. Mr. Cooper has a hearty faith in the good sense and patriotism of the American people, when questions affecting the safety and honor of the republic are fairly put before them. He, himself, has only a common education, a common sense, and an earnest American patriotism to bring to bear on these questions of public policy. He, therefore, appeals to the American people from the common standpoint of thought and feeling which belongs to all, and gives his views in a plain and hearty manner, "with good will to all, and with malice toward none."

Above all, Mr. Cooper desires three principles of political and financial prosperity to be made an essential part of the Constitution and laws of the republic, in order to secure it permanence and happiness:

First, A tariff not simply for revenue, but made *discriminating* and helpful to all the industries of the country, where the raw material and the labor can be furnished by our own people.

Second, A national paper currency, issued solely by the Government, and made the only legal tender, receivable for all taxes and dues, and fundable at any time for an equitable rate of interest, by being made *interconvertible* with the bonds of the Government.

The *volume* of this currency must be determined by law, as *per capita*.

The *value* of this currency is determined by the rate of interest given by the interconvertible bond, and by its *indispensable* use for paying all debts, taxes, and dues that can be collected by law.

The *convertibility* of this paper currency is secured by *bonds* " as good as gold," and by keeping its *volume* and its *value* at that point where its unit measure, or *standard* of value, requires it to represent a certain amount of weight and fineness in gold or silver, " *dollar for dollar.*"   In other words, we want, *as far as possible*, an *unfluctuating* currency, both in volume and value ; but Mr. Cooper thinks that such a currency cannot be obtained by making *coin* the sole legal tender and money of the country, and paper merely its *representative*.   This paper can be made to represent all values *directly*, and not *circuitously*, through coin, by being made to represent the highest and most indispensable use of money—namely, to pay taxes, dues, debts, and to command *interest*, or secure an *income*.   What can any " bullionist" desire of good money more than this—that it should be as "good as gold," and accomplish all that money is used for ?

This is what Mr. Cooper desires to accomplish for our " national currency."

Thirdly, Mr. Cooper earnestly desires a " civil service " divorced from party politics, and organized for the public service, as are the departments of the army or navy, purely on personal qualification and thorough fitness.   The offices to be held during good behavior, on *moderate salaries*, but pensions provided for all disqualified by age or sickness, and a provision made for the widows and orphans.

These are the simple principles of administration which Mr. Cooper offers as his thorough and warm convictions.   He hopes to make this little book one of the most useful, as it may be the last of those contributions to the welfare and progress of his beloved country, to which his best hopes and efforts have been devoted through a long life of eighty-seven years.

J. C. ZACHOS, EDITOR.

NEW YORK, July 28, 1877.

EARLY DAYS AND BUSINESS LIFE

OF

PETER COOPER.

An Autobiography.

CHAPTER I.

THE EARLY DAYS AND BUSINESS LIFE OF PETER COOPER.

PETER COOPER was born in the city of New York, February 12th, 1791. He comes from a family distinguished for their unwavering devotion to the cause of American Independence. His maternal grandfather, John Cambell, was Alderman of New York, and Deputy Quartermaster during the war. He sacrificed a large fortune in the cause of his country's freedom, and had nothing but a large quantity of "Continental money," as an acknowledgment. Mr. Cooper often laughs at this "paper payment," but says, "it was precious stuff, after all, for it was an essential means of our gaining our Independence." He thinks it very unfair and illogical, however, to quote "Continental money," and "French assignats," against his theory of a national paper legal tender, for both the former were allowed to remain irredeemable and inconvertible (the land conversion being made impossible), whereas he desires a currency which is both a legal tender and *interconvertible* into Government bonds at the will of the holder. His father was lieutenant in the patriot army, and at the close of the war returned to New York, where he engaged in business.

The early part of Mr. Cooper's life is best told in his own simple and conversational language, obtained in many conversations with the author, and characterized by that homely directness of statement of facts, which like Defoe's "Robinson Crusoe," gives wonderful charm to the life and character that pervade the facts.

HIS FATHER AND MOTHER.

"My father, after the Revolutionary war, had done a successful business in the manufacture of hats in the City of New York; and when I was about three years old, he, like many others, became enamoured with a country life, and bought a place at Peekskill, built a store there, carried on the business of a country store-keeper, and built a church. He found plenty of custom all over the country that would buy on credit, and it was not more than two or three years before he found that nearly all of his property was in the hands of other people, and

1

that it was impossible for him to collect it. He believed devoutly that I should 'come to something;' for he named me Peter, after the great Apostle, and maintained that he was told to do so in a sort of 'waking vision.' My mother was an excellent woman, and did the best she could with a large family, narrow circumstances, and a changing home.

"My father followed the business of a hatter, and the first I remember was being utilized in this business by being set to pull the hair out of rabbit skins, when my head was just above the table. I remained in this business until I could make every part of a hat. My father finally sold out his hatter's business to my eldest brother, by a former wife, and commenced the brewing of ale in the town of Peekskill. It was my business to deliver the kegs of ale to the different places in town and country where it had been sold. Finding this a 'slow business' my father bought a place at Catskill, where he commenced again the hatter's business, and also that of making bricks. I was made useful in this business in carrying and handling the bricks for the drying process.

"My father at length finding that his business at Catskill did not answer his expectations, sold out and removed to Brooklyn, N. Y.

"Here I worked again at the hatter's business with my father until again he sold out and bought some property in Newburg, N. Y., on which he erected a brewery. At this business I continued with my father until I was seventeen.

"The only time I ever trusted to chance for any profit, was about this time, when I got a very wholesome lesson. I had earned about ten dollars beyond my immediate wants, which I invested, by the advice of a relative, in lottery tickets, all which, fortunately for me, drew blanks. This impressed upon me the folly of looking to games of chance for any source of gain or livelihood.

HIS APPRENTICESHIP.

"In my seventeenth year I entered as apprentice to the coach-making business. I remained in this four years, till I was of age, and had thoroughly learned the business. During my apprenticeship I received twenty-five dollars a year for my services; to this sum I added something by working at night at coach carving, and such other work as I could get. My grandmother gave me the use of a room, in one of her rear buildings on Broadway, where I spent much of my time in nightly work, instead of going with other apprentices who too often went with loose companions and contracted habits that proved their ruin. One such example impressed itself very strongly on my mind at that time.

It was that of a young man who literally rotted and died of disease before he was sixteen years of age.

"During my apprenticeship I made for my employer a machine for mortising the hubs of carriages, which proved very profitable to him, and was, perhaps, the first of its kind used in this country.

"When I was twenty-one years old, my employer offered to build me a shop and set me up in business, but as I always had a horror of being burdened with debt, and having no capital of my own, I declined his kind offer.

THE MACHINE FOR SHEARING CLOTH.

"As soon as I was of age I went to the town of Hempstead, L. I., to see my brother. Here I was persuaded to work for a man at the making of machines for shearing cloth. I continued at this for three years, for a dollar and fifty cents a day, which was regarded as very large wages at that time. I saved enough at the end of my engagement to buy the right of the State of New York for a machine for shearing cloth, and I commenced the manufacture of these machines on my own account. This business proved very successful. The first money I received for the sale of my machines was from Mr. Vassar, of Poughkeepsie, who afterwards founded that noble institution for female education, called the Vassar College, at Poughkeepsie. My sales to Mr. Vassar also included one of the patent rights for the county in which he resided. This put in my possession so large an amount of money according to my ideas at that time, about five hundred dollars, that I was very much elated and rejoiced at what I considered my great good fortune. But my joy was soon turned to mourning. On my return from Poughkeepsie I visited my father, who lived then at Newburg. I found the family in the deepest affliction on account of the pressure of debts which my father was unable to pay. The money I had just received for my machines enabled me to pay the most pressing of these debts, and left me barely the means to purchase materials to commence the making of new machines. Besides this, I became surety for my father for debts not yet matured, which I paid as they fell due, and in consequence of this my father never had the mortification of failing in business. The same is true in my own affairs, notwithstanding some public statements made to the contrary by persons ignorant of the facts.

"So far from ever having failed in business, I do not remember the week or month when every man who has ever worked for me did not get his pay when it was due. This is strictly true, through a business life of more than sixty years, in which I have had at times, as many as twenty-five hundred people in my employment.

"The coach-making business, I never followed after serving out my apprenticeship. But soon after I commenced the manufacture of machines for shearing cloth, I made an improvement that enabled me to sell these machines as fast as I could make them. At this time they were in great demand, in consequence of the war of 1812 with England, which stopped our commerce with that country. At the close of the war, however, this business lost its value, and I gave it up.

"It is worth while to mention here that the principle and method of my machine for shearing cloth was precisely the one now used so largely in mowing and reaping machines; and this was so obvious that a gentleman seeing my machine at work suggested that a similar machine might be made for mowing grass, and asked me to make for him a model for this purpose. This was operated for the purpose of cutting the grass in his yard, and proved entirely successful, long before any machine for mowing had been invented or patented by others.

COMMENCES MERCANTILE BUSINESS.

"After some three years' continuance in this business of manufacture, I bought a twenty-years' lease of two houses and six lots of ground where the 'Bible House' now stands, opposite the Cooper Union. On this ground I erected four wooden dwelling-houses. I was engaged at this time in the grocery business, in which I continued for three years.

"Soon after this, I purchased a glue factory, with all its stock and buildings, on a lease of twenty-one years, for three acres of ground, on what was then known as the "old middle road," between Thirty-first and Thirty-fourth streets. Here I continued to manufacture glue, oil, whiting, prepared chalk, and isinglass to the end of my lease. I then bought ten acres of ground on Maspeth avenue, Brooklyn, where the business has continued to the present time.

"What I made by building machines and in the grocery business had enabled me to pay for the glue factory on the day of the purchase.

THE BALTIMORE RAILROAD AND THE FIRST LOCOMOTIVE IN THE COUNTRY.

"In 1828 I purchased three thousand acres of land within the city limits of Baltimore for one hundred and five thousand dollars ($105,000). On a part of that property, I erected the Canton Iron Works, which, afterwards, I sold to Mr. Abott, of Baltimore. I was drawn into this speculation in Baltimore, by two men who represented that they had large means, and we bought together three thousand acres of land in the city of Baltimore for one hundred and five thousand dollars ($105,000), taking the whole shore from Fell's Point dock for three miles. After paying my part of the money, I soon found that I had paid all that had been paid upon the property, and that I was even paying the board of the two men who had agreed to take part in the purchase. Finding that to be the situation, I was compelled to say to them that they must pay their part or sell out, or buy me out. Neither of them having the ability to buy, I finally succeeded in getting them to state a price; one offered to go out for ten thousand dollars ($10,000), the other for a smaller sum; which offers I accepted and bought them out.

"When we first purchased the property it was in the midst of a great excitement created by a promise of the rapid completion of the Baltimore and Ohio Railroad, which had been commenced by a subscription of five dollars per share. In the course of the first year's operations they had spent more than the five dollars per share. But the road had to make so many short turns in going around points of rocks that they found they could not complete the road without a much larger sum than they had supposed would be necessary; while the many short turns in the road seemed to render it entirely useless for locomotive purposes. The principal stockholders had become so discouraged that they said, they would not pay any more, and would lose all they had already paid in. After conversing with them, I told them that if they would hold on a little while, I would put a small locomotive on the road, which I thought would demonstrate the practicability of using steam-engines on the road, even with all the short turns in it. I got up a small engine for that purpose, and put it on the road, and invited the stockholders to witness the experiment. After a great deal of trouble and difficulty in accomplishing the work, the stockholders came, and thirty-six men were taken into a car, and, with six men on the locomotive, which carried its own fuel and water, and having to go up hill eighteen feet to a mile, and turn all the short turns around the points of rocks, we succeeded in making the thirteen miles, on the first passage out, in one hour and twelve minutes; and we returned from Ellicott's Mills to Baltimore in fifty-seven minutes.

"This locomotive was built to demonstrate that cars could be drawn around short curves, beyond anything believed in at that time to be possible. The success of this locomotive also answered the question of the possibility of building railroads in a country scarce of capital, and with immense stretches of very rough country to pass, in order to connect commercial centres, without the deep cuts, the tunnelling, and levelling which short curves might avoid. My contrivance saved this road from bankruptcy.

THE IRON WORKS.

"The discouragement and stoppage of progress in improvement in the city of Baltimore that had been occasioned by the state of things in the Baltimore and Ohio Railroad made it difficult to do anything with the property before mentioned but to keep it ; and in order to make it pay something towards meeting the cost, taxes, etc., I determined to build iron works upon it. I had four or five hundred tons of iron ore raised, dug, etc., at Lazaretto Point, and I determined to cut the wood off of the property, which was being stolen in every direction, and to burn it into charcoal, and use it up in making charcoal iron. For which purpose I built a rolling-mill, which I afterwards sold to Mr. Abbot. In my efforts to make iron, I had to commence to burn the wood into charcoal, and in order to do that, I erected large kilns, twenty-five feet in diameter, twelve feet high, circular in form, hooped around with iron at the top, arched over so as to make a tight place in which to put the wood, with single bricks left out in different places in order to smother the fire out when the wood was sufficiently burned.

A NARROW ESCAPE.

"After having burned the coal in one of these kilns very perfectly, and believing the fire entirely smothered out, we attempted to take the coal out of the kiln; but when we had got it about half-way out, the coal itself took fire, and the men, after carrying water for some time to extinguish it, gave up in despair. I then went myself to the door of the kiln to see if anything more could be done, and just as I entered the door the gas itself took fire, and enveloped me in a sheet of flame.

"I had to run some ten feet to get out, and in doing so my eyebrows and whiskers were burned, and my fur hat was scorched down to the body of the fur. How I escaped I know not. I seemed to be literally blown out by the explosion, and I narrowly escaped with my life.

FIRST GREAT SUCCESSFUL OPERATION.

"After seeing the difficulties that attended the making of iron there, I determined, having so large a property on my hands, to sell it for what I could get, and at the first offer made. I succeeded in getting an offer of nearly what it had cost me from two men from Boston, Amos Binney and Edmund Monroe. They formed out of the property what is now known as the Canton Co. I took a considerable portion of my pay in stock, at forty-four dollars the share—par value one hundred dollars. I reserved the iron works sold to Mr. Abbot; and, as good luck would have it, the stock commenced rising almost at once, as soon as it was put into form, and continued to go up in the market until it attained the enormous figure of two hundred and thirty dollars per share. This enabled me to sell out my stock to a very great advantage, so that I made money by the operation.

"I then returned to my old business in New York, and after one or two years, built the iron factory in Thirty-third street near Third avenue. I leased it to a man who had it for one or two years and failed, and I had to take it off his hands. I turned it into a rolling mill for rolling iron and making wire, and ran it for some years.

"I then removed it to Trenton, N. J., where I bought water power to carry the works on, and enlarged the works by building a mill and a wire factory. A few years later I built three large blast furnaces at Phillipsburg, the largest then known, near Easton, Penn.; bought the Andover mines, and built a railroad through a rough country for eight miles, to bring the ore down to the furnaces, at the rate of 40,000 tons a year. After running the works for several years I was induced to form them into a company called the Trenton Iron Works, including the rolling-mills and the blast furnaces, and 11,000 acres known as the Ringwood property. I had built a second rolling-mill and wire factory in Trenton, which was also included in the company. I sold one half of these works in the formation of the company. This continued for a number of years, when a division was made, and the company took one part of the property, the blast furnaces, and I took the rolling-mills and the Ringwood property. This property is still in the family.

"During all this time I had continued the manufacture of glue, isinglass, oil, prepared chalk, Paris white, and also the grinding of white lead, and fulling of buckskins, for the manufacture of buckskin leather.

"It was in one of those mills above mentioned, that the first iron beams were rolled, now so much used in fire-proof buildings. In planning the building of the Cooper Union I desired to make it fire-proof as far as possible, and found no such iron beams could be obtained. I determined to have them rolled at one of my mills; but found, in the end, that the necessary experiments and suitable machinery had cost me seventy-five thousand dollars. It has proved, however, a profitable business since."

THE LAYING OF THE OCEAN CABLE.

A very interesting episode in Mr. Cooper's life was the interest he took, and the personal efforts he made in behalf of that most important and difficult of modern enterprises, the laying of an ocean cable.

It is not too much to say, that to the perseverance, energy, and unconquerable faith of Mr. Cooper and two or three others, whom he mentions, we owe that great gift to modern progress and civilization.

I have often heard the narrative from his lips, and give it very much in his own words:

"It is now twenty years since I became the President of the North American Telegraph Company, when it controlled more than one-half of all the lines then in the country; also President of the New York, Newfoundland, and London Telegraph Company.

"An attempt had been made to put a line of telegraph across Newfoundland, on which some work had been done. Cyrus W. Field, Moses Taylor, Marshal O. Roberts, Wilson G. Hunt, and myself completed that work across the island of Newfoundland, and then laid a cable across the Gulf of St. Lawrence, intending it as the beginning of a line from Europe to America by telegraphic communication. After one form of difficulty after another had been surmounted, we found that more than ten years had passed before we got a cent in return, and we had been spending money the whole time. We lost the first cable laid, which cost some three or four hundred thousand dollars, at the Gulf of St. Lawrence, which loss was occasioned by the seeming determination of the captain of the ship that towed our vessel across the Gulf to have his own way, in opposition to the directions of Mr. Buchanan, who directed him to keep a certain flag in sight as far as he could see it, in connection with a certain mark on the top of a mountain, which was visible nearly half way across the Gulf.

"We had hired a vessel at seven hundred and fifty dollars a day, and we directed the steamer *Adger* to go to Cape Ray, and tow the vessel across the Gulf, in order to lay the cable. We went to Port Basque, and found the vessel had not arrived. We accordingly anchored in

Port Basque until she did arrive, which was two days later. On her arrival, the captain was directed to take our vessel in tow, and carry her up to Cape Ray, where we had already prepared a telegraph house, from which to commence laying the cable. On this telegraph house we placed a flag-staff, which was to be kept in line by the steamer, as she crossed the Gulf, with a certain very excellent landmark on the top of a mountain some three, four, or five miles distant—a landmark which seemed to be made on purpose for our use.

"We had an accident at starting. We joined the ends of the cable and brought one end into the telegraph house, and made everything ready to take the vessel in tow. The captain was then directed to bring his steamer in line, take the vessel in tow, and carry her across the Gulf. In doing that he ran his steamer into the vessel, carried away her shrouds and quarter-rail, and almost ruined our enterprise the first thing, dragging the cable over the stern of the vessel with such force as to break the connection; and we were obliged to cut the cable and splice it again. The captain of the steamer had failed entirely in trying to get hold of the vessel; and after we had mended the cable, and got everything ready for a second attempt, he was again ordered to take the vessel in tow. We had provided ourselves with two large cables, two hundred feet long and four inches in diameter, as tow-lines, so as to be sure of having sufficient strength to tow the vessel in all kinds of weather; but the captain of the steamer so managed matters, in his second attempt to take the vessel in tow, as to get this cable entangled in the steamer's wheel, and he hallooed to the captain of the vessel to let his cable slip, in order to get this unentangled. At this, the captain of the vessel let go his cable and lost his anchor and one of our big cables, for we had to cut it, in order to disentangle it from the wheel. After that was got loose there was the vessel without an anchor, and she was going rapidly down upon a reef of rocks, with a strong wind against her. It was only with the greatest difficulty that we could get the captain of the *Adger* to go to her relief, and save her from being dashed on the rocks, with her forty men on board. We had to expostulate with the captain of the steamer until the vessel was within two or three hundred feet of the rocks, before he would consent to attempt her rescue; and by the merest good luck, we got out a rope to her and saved her from going on the rocks, when she was so close to the shore that we could almost have thrown a line there.

"The captain of the steamer, however, got hold of the vessel at last, and brought her back to her place in the harbor, where we had to renew the connection of our cable, and prepare again to start.

"The third attempt to take hold of the vessel was successful, and on a beautiful morning we started to lay the cable across the Gulf.

"In a very little while I discovered that we were getting out of line with the marks that the captain had been directed to steer by. As President of the line, I called the matter to the attention of the captain. The answer I got was: 'I know how to steer my ship; I steer by my compass.' It went on a little while longer, and finding that he was still going farther out of the line, I called his attention to the fact again, and so on, again and again, for some time, until he had got some eight or ten miles out of the line. I then said to him, 'Captain, we shall have to hold you responsible for the loss of this cable!' We got a lawyer on board to draw up a paper to present to him, stating that we should hold him responsible for the loss of the cable, as he had not obeyed the orders of Mr. Buchanan, as agreed on. After we had served this paper upon him, he turned the course of his ship, and went just as far from the line in the other direction. He had also agreed not to let his vessel go more than a mile and a half an hour, as it was impossible, under the circumstances, to pay out the cable faster than a mile and a half an hour. It was discovered, however, that he was running his vessel faster and faster, while Mr. Buchanan hallooed, 'Slower! slower!' until finally the captain got a kink in the cable, and was obliged to stop. This happened several times.

"So much delay took place that when it was late in the afternoon, we had not laid over forty miles of the cable out of the eighty miles that we had to go in crossing the Gulf. Then a very severe gale came up, and raged with such violence that the steamer *Victoria*, which was a small one, came near being swamped; and in order to save that vessel, and the forty men on board of her, we were compelled to cut the cable.

"Subsequently, we sent a vessel to take up that part of the cable; and it was then found that we had payed out twenty-four miles of cable, and had gone only nine miles from shore! We had spent so much money, and lost so much time, that it was very vexatious to us to have our enterprise defeated in the way it was, by the stupidity and obstinacy of one man. This man was one of the rebels that fired the first guns upon Fort Sumter. The poor fellow is now dead.

"Having lost this cable, we ordered another, and had it ready in a year or two. This time we had a good man to put it down, and we had no trouble with it.

"The great question then came up: What could we do about an ocean cable? After getting a few subscriptions here, which did not amount to much, we sent Mr. Field across the ocean, to see if he could get the balance of the subscriptions in England; and he succeeded, to the astonishment of almost everybody, because we had been set down as crazy people, spending our money as if it had been water. Mr. Field succeeded in getting the amount wanted, and in contracting for a cable. It was put on two ships which were to meet in mid-ocean. They did meet, joined the two ends of the cable, and laid it down successfully. We brought our end to Newfoundland, where we received over it some four hundred messages. · Very soon after it started, however, we found it began to fail, and it grew weaker and weaker, until at length it could not be understood any more.

"It so happened that the few messages that we received over the cable were important to the English Government, for it had arranged to transport a large number of soldiers from Canada to China, in the war with the Chinese, and just before the transports were to make sail a telegram came stating that peace was declared. This inspired the people of England with confidence in our final success. This occurred just before the Crystal Palace burned down, and we had a meeting in the Crystal Palace to celebrate the great triumph of having received and sent messages across the ocean. .Our triumph was short-lived, for it was only a few days after that the cable had so weakened in transmitting that it could no longer be understood.

"One-half the people did not now believe that we had ever had any messages across the cable. It was all a humbug, they thought. In the Chamber of Commerce the question came up about a telegraph line, and a man got up and said: 'It is all a humbug! No message ever came over!' At that, Mr. Cunard arose, and said that 'the gentleman did not know what he was talking about, and had no right to say what he had, and that he himself had sent messages and got the answers.'

"Mr. Cunard was a positive witness; he had been on the spot; and the man must have felt 'slim' at the result of his attempt to cast ridicule on men whose efforts, if unsuccessful, were at least not unworthy of praise.

"We succeeded in getting another cable, but when we had got it about half-way over, we lost that as well. Then the question seemed hopeless. We thought for a long time that our money was all lost. The matter rested some two years before anything more was done. My friend Mr. Wilson G. Hunt, used to talk to me often about it; for we had brought him into the Board some two or three years before. He said he did not feel much interest in it, but he felt concerned about spending so much money; and he remarked that he was not sure, as we had spent so much money already about the telegraph line, but that we had better spend a little more. So we sent Mr. Field out again. We had spent so much money already, it was 'like pulling teeth' out of Roberts and Taylor to get more money from them; but we got up the sum necessary to send Mr. Field out.

"When he arrived there, Mr. Field said they laughed at him for thinking of getting up another cable. They said that they thought the thing was dead enough, and buried deep enough in the ocean to satisfy anybody. But Mr. Field was not satisfied. Finally he got hold of an old Quaker friend, who was a very rich man, and he so completely electrified him with the idea of the work, that he put three or four hundred thousand dollars into it immediately to lay another cable, and in fourteen days after Mr. Field had got that man's name, he had the whole amount of subscriptions made up, six millions of dollars.

"The cable was made and put down, and it worked successfully. We then went out to see if we could not pick up the other one. The balance of the lost cable was on board the ship. The cable was found, picked up, and joined to the rest—and this wonder of the world was accomplished. - I do not think that feat is surpassed by any other human achievement. The cable was taken out of water, two and a half miles deep, in mid-ocean. It was pulled up three times, before it was saved. They got it up just far enough to see it, and it would go down again, and they would have to do the work over again. They used up all their coal, and spent ten or twelve days in 'hooking' for the cable before it was finally caught. But they succeeded; the two ends of the cable were brought in connection, and then we had two complete cables across the ocean.

"In taking up the first cable the cause of the failure was discovered. It originated in the manufacture of the cable. In passing the cable into the vat provided for it, where it was intended to lie under water all the time, until put aboard the ship, the workmen neglected to keep the water at all times over the cable; and on one occasion, when the sun shone very hotly down into this vat where the cable was lying uncovered, its rays melted the gutta percha, so that the copper wire inside, sunk down against the outer covering. I have a piece of the cable which shows just how it occurred. The first cable that was laid would have been a perfect success, if it had not been for that error in manufacturing it. The copper wire sagged down against the outside covering, and there was just a thin layer of gutta percha to prevent it from coming in contact with the water. In building the first cables their philosophy was not so well understood as it is now; and so, when the cable began to fail, they increased the power of the battery; and it is supposed that a spark of the electricity came in contact with water, and the electricity passed off into the water.

"After the two ocean cables had been laid successfully, it was found necessary to have a second cable across the Gulf of St. Lawrence. Our delays had been so trying and unfortunate in the past, that none of the stockholders, with the exception of Mr. Field, Mr. Taylor, Mr. Roberts, and myself, would take any interest in the matter. We had to get the money by offering bonds, which we had power to do by charter; and these were offered at fifty cents on the dollar. Mr. Field, Mr. Roberts, Mr. Taylor, and myself were compelled to take up the principal part of the stock at that rate, in order to get the necessary funds. We had to do the business through the Bank of Newfoundland, and the bank would not trust the company, but drew personally on me. I told them to draw on the company, but they continued to draw on me, and I had to pay the drafts or let them go back protested. I was often out ten or twenty thousand dollars in advance, in that way, to keep the thing going. After the cable became a success, the stock rose to ninety dollars per share, at which figure we sold out to an English company. That proved to be the means of saving us from loss. The work was finished at last, and I never have regretted it, although it was a terrible time to go through.

CHAPTER II.

THE INVENTIVE LIFE AND ENTERPRISES OF MR. COOPER.

MR. COOPER'S mind is not one of great invention, but a mind of great contrivance. He lacks the elementary training in the principles of mechanics and constructive drawing, which accurately guide the mind through the labyrinths of great inventions, and lead it safely to the end. In truth, most inventions, so called, are mere contrivances for the improved application of old inventions.

Mr. Cooper's sound good sense and practical knowledge have always directed his invention to some immediate useful result connected with his own private business, or some object of public interest. But, on the whole, he has met with more than the average degree of success of "those who make many inventions."

As this is a sort of "autobiography written by another," we will give a brief account of some of these inventions and contrivances of Mr. Cooper, as obtained from him in conversation. They certainly exhibit a thoroughly American mind, full of expedients and inventive resources for making the most of what God and nature put into his hands. Some of Mr. Cooper's important inventions have already been mentioned as part of his business life.

Mr. Cooper says: "I very early took to making and contriving for myself or friends. I remember one of the earliest things I undertook, of my own accord, was to make a pair of shoes. For this purpose I first obtained an old pair, and took them all apart to see the structure; and then, procuring leather, thread, needles, and some suitable tools, without further instruction, I made the last and a pair of shoes, which compared very well with the country shoes then in vogue."

"When I was an apprentice to the business of carriage-making, I spent all my spare time in ornamental carving in an upper room which my grandmother gave me for this purpose, on Broadway. This was my occupation, instead of walking the streets or going to places of public resort, as other apprentices of my age. I made for my employer at that time, a machine for mortising the hubs of wheels, which proved very profitable to him, and induced him afterwards to offer to set me up in the business of carriage-making.

THE TIDE-WATER USED AS A POWER.

" When I was an apprentice at the coach-making business I planned
out and made at night a model machine to show how power could
be obtained from the natural current of the tide, and be applied to
various useful purposes. My model represented a plan for causing the
water-wheel to rise and fall with the tide, at any desired speed, by the
action of its own machinery. It was so arranged that the whole power
could be thrown on a saw-mill or be made to force compressed air into
a reservoir, to be used as a motive power to propel ferry-boats across
the river. This was to be done by making the hull of a ferry-boat to
consist of two strong iron cylinders, to form the buoyancy of the boat,
and a reservoir of power to drive a boat across the river. On these
cylinders, I placed, at a sufficient distance apart to receive the water or
driving-wheel, either between the cylinders or on the outside, as might
be thought most convenient, the deck to rest on and be fastened to
these cylinders or reservoirs for power.

" The power was to be received from a reservoir of compressed air on
the dock, by connecting the hull of the boat with the reservoir by means
of a flexible tube, when in the dock, at every trip. The air to be worked
off by its expansion and pressure, similar to the working of a steam-
engine.

" The wreck of the old tide-mill is still in the garret of my house.

" I remember that Fulton did me the honor to come and see my model
and machinery, but he was too much occupied at that time with his own
plans of steamboat navigation, to pay much attention to my invention."

ROTARY MOTION OBTAINED FROM RECTILINEAR ALTERNATING MOTION, WITHOUT A CRANK.

" I had read from the books, or heard said, that there was no loss of
power communicated through a crank, except from friction. I doubted
this. There are two 'dead points' in the crank motion, which nothing
but the inertia of a fly-wheel or something equivalent, can overcome. I
made an experiment to show that the rectilinear motion of a piston-rod
could produce the rotary motion of an axle with less loss of power
than through a crank.

" By special contrivance, I made my piston-rod a part of the circuit of
an endless chain, which went around the circumference of a driving-
wheel, and communicated power without any crank. It would be
difficult to describe this machine without drawings, but the result was

that I proved to the satisfaction of the City Engineer, against his former convictions, that there was a loss of power in the use of the crank, and I gained, with my application of the reciprocal and rectilinear motion of the piston-rod, a power which was as five to eight over the crank.

"I made a small engine on this principle, and used it in the 'first locomotive,' which I have spoken of before, on the Ohio and Baltimore Railroad, making a trial trip with the President alone. But before I came to try it with the train of cars, it was so unskilfully handled by some meddlesome person that it broke twice, and I was obliged, at last, in that experiment, to put a cross-head and crank on the engine. I have the remains of that first model of the engine in my garret yet."

A METHOD OF PROPULSION ON THE ERIE CANAL.

Mr. Cooper said: "Fifty-three years ago, a year before the water was let into the Erie canal, it occurred to me that canal-boats might be propelled by the force of water drawn from a higher level, and made to move a series of endless chains along the course of the canal. So I began to make experiments. I built a flat-bottomed scow, took a couple of men, and choosing that part of the East River that lies between what is now the foot of Eighth street and where Bellevue Hospital now stands —a distance of one mile—I drove posts into the mud, one hundred feet apart. On these posts I fastened rollers made of block tin and zinc, on which my endless chain could run. There were two rollers on each post, one above the other, so that the chain could run up on one roller and back on the other. Then I made two miles of chain. Here is a piece of it now."

The old gentleman took from the drawer three or four links of the chain, rusty with age. They were of large iron wire,.each link about five inches long, rudely twisted together, something like a surveyor's chain.

"This chain is of four-horse power," continued Mr. Cooper. "I tested it. I then arranged a water-wheel to run the chain. This preparation took a deal of time, for I did most of the work myself. When it was completed, I took a small skiff, fastened my tow line to the chain, started my wheel, and found that the experiment was a success. I invited Gov. Clinton and a few other gentlemen to make a trip. We ran the two miles, up and back, in eleven minutes. The Governor was so well pleased that he paid me eight hundred dollars for the privilege of purchasing the patent right for the use of the canal.

"It was never used on the canal, and for this reason : Gov. Clinton had great difficulty in getting the farmers on the line of the canal to give him the right of way, and in order to induce them to grant it had held out to them the great advantages that would arise to them of selling their oats, corn, hay, and other produce to the canal men for the use of the horses. If the endless chain was used, these promises would be good for nothing, as there would be no horses to feed. So Gov. Clinton gave up my scheme. I ran the chain on the river for ten days, during which time hundreds of people made the trip. At the end of that time I took the chain off the river. Well, the matter stood still until a few years ago Mr. Weltch, the President of the Camden and Amboy Canal Company, hit upon the endless chain plan for getting his boats through the locks. He tried it, and it worked well. So he went to Washington to take out a patent, and found on searching the records that I had taken out a patent on the very same invention, fifty years before. Of course my patent had run out, so the invention was free to all."

MECHANICAL TRANSPORTATION BY THE FORCE OF GRAVITY.

Mr. Cooper has often resorted to his contrivance in saving the expense of labor, when labor was both scarce and dear. Two instances of his ingenuity are thus related by himself:

"It is about twelve years since I made an endless band of round iron, near three-eighths of an inch in diameter, extending in the form of a belt for about three miles, for the purpose of transporting coal from the mines to my furnaces. This belt of iron was supported on wheels fastened to posts, the wheels having grooved surfaces to support the belt. On this belt I fastened buckets formed to receive iron ore. These buckets, when filled with ore, were on a descending grade sufficient to carry the ore down and return the empty buckets.

"During the time I owned the Canton property, I made a belt of cars which I placed on a double track railroad. One track was held right over the other in a frame for the purpose. The belt of cars was placed on a double track railroad in this framework, and was intended to transport by its own weight, a sand-bank into Harris Creek bottom, which I desired then to fill up. The framework with its rails and belt of cars, was placed on longitudinal sleepers, so as to be moved up to the side of the bank, as the sand was being removed. The sand could be carelessly thrown into a long hopper, over the cars, on the upper track. The cars, after dumping their load at the lower end, returned on the lower track, bottom upwards, to be constantly refilled."

2

THE TORPEDO VESSEL FOR THE GREEKS.

The only "bloody-minded thing" that Mr. Cooper ever made was a torpedo-boat, designed to blow the Turks out of water, for their inhuman cruelties to the Greeks, in the struggle to regain their freedom. This was about 1824 or 1825.

Mr. Cooper relates, with some mirthfulness, how he was "perfectly indignant" at the conduct of the Turks, and had his "sympathies, in common with many of his fellow-citizens, greatly excited in behalf of the struggling Greeks;" so he determined to take up their cause in a very destructive way. "I planned a torpedo-boat, which might be sent from shore, or from a vessel towards an enemy's ship six or eight miles off. The torpedo-boat was to be propelled by a screw and a steam-engine, and guided and directed towards its object by a couple of steel wires six or eight miles long, unwound from a suitable reel, and adjusted to the steering apparatus of the boat. I tried these wires first on a small steamer that I directed in the Harbor, near the Narrows, and they worked very well for six miles, until another boat came across my wires and broke them. When ready for service, I designed to place red-hot cannon balls in the boiler of my engine, to furnish the steam. The torpedo being placed on a bent piece of iron projecting far from the bow of my boat, when it struck the enemy the shock would explode the torpedo and bend the piece of iron, and by a proper contrivance reverse the action of the engine, and send the boat back again, guided and directed by the wires. I was preparing this torpedo-boat to go with the ship which our citizens were about to send, with provisions, clothing, and medicines, to the unfortunate victims of the Turkish war, and I designed it to be the "bitterest pill" in the whole cargo; but unfortunately, I did not get it ready in time, and it was soon after burned up in my factory, with all the rest of the contents."

THE MUSICAL, MECHANICAL ROCKING-CRADLE.

Mr. Cooper was always very kind and indulgent in his domestic relations, and delighted in the society of his wife and children. He says, "In early life, when I was first married, I found it necessary to 'rock the cradle,' while my wife prepared our frugal meals. This was not always convenient, in my busy life, and I conceived the idea of making a cradle that would be made to rock by a mechanism. I did so, and enlarging upon my first idea, I arranged the mechanism for keeping off the flies, and playing a music-box for the amusement of the baby! This cradle was bought of me afterwards, by a delighted pedlar, who gave me his 'whole stock in trade' for the exchange and the privilege of selling the patent in the State of Connecticut."

MR. COOPER'S WIFE AND FAMILY.

Here we will say a few words with regard to Mr. Cooper's wife and family relations.

Mr. Cooper married Miss Sarah Bedel, of Hempstead, Long Island, in December, 1813, being then twenty-two years old, and his wife in her twenty-first year. They had six children, four of whom died in childhood. The two children surviving are Edward Cooper, of the firm of Cooper & Hewitt, merchants in New York city; and Mrs. Sarah Amelia Hewitt, wife of the Hon. A. S. Hewitt, Member of Congress.

Mrs. Cooper died in the seventy-seventh year of her age, and on the fifty-sixth anniversary of her wedding day, December, 1869.

Mr. Cooper never speaks of his wife without emotion. He attributes all his highest happiness, and most of his success in life, to the sterling qualities of character in his wife. He says, she was the "day star, the solace and the inspiration of his life,"—words that express a deep feeling, and also a substantial fact; for there is no doubt, from the character given her by others, that she was a woman of superior moral qualities, and had precisely that fitness and training that made a worthy and most efficient "help-mate" of Mr. Cooper. Certain it is, that her position was one of no secondary importance in Mr. Cooper's life and the development of his character. We give, therefore, a few extracts from Dr. Bellows' sermon at her funeral services, which, though in stately language, gives a fine and truthful analysis of the character of Mrs. Cooper.

"Born in respectable circumstances, of honest blood, reared to industry and self-denial, her providential lot united her at an early period to the husband whose blessed companion she has been for more than half a century. His toils and anxieties she shared during the long, patient, persistent struggle with the difficulties that always beset self-made fortune and self-made men and women; his home she ordered and brightened, and enriched with her native industry, fidelity, and cheerfulness; his judgment she steadied by her weighty good sense; his prosperity she helped to keep modest and unpretending; his beneficence proceeded in no small part from the results of her prudence and economy, and from the fixed habit of serviceableness to others, which had its root in her essential goodness of heart, but was confirmed by practice, enlightened by experience, and perfected by religious principles.

"God alone can sum up and estimate the value of a life characteristically unselfish from beginning to end, in which, to human observation, every throb of the heart has been in the interest of virtue and goodness. Who but He can measure the worth of nearly eighty years of spotless fidelity to truth and ceaseless devotion to duty—each year, each month, each day, each hour, recording its noiseless act of self-control, forbearance with others, training and counsel for children, sympathy and support for husband and friend; action, solicitude for sorrowing, sick, and tempted neighbors; steady provision for the pleasure and profit of humble dependents; a hand open to its fullest extent, and a heart tender and full of sincere charity and peace with all the world.

.   .   .   .

"Strife and discontent, disorder and murmurs, could not live long in her gentle presence. Like sunshine in a shady place, she banished the damps of worldly care and the poisonous dews of envy and jealousy. Her household gathered around her as we gather from the winter's cold about the genial fireside. Her generous, outgrowing heart and ready love melted the frosts of custom and the snows of formality and all the icicles of glittering pride away. It was impossible to be artificial, false, pretentious in her sincere and simple presence. And how full and steady and strong the love she gave and drew towards her! To-day, the fifty-sixth anniversary of her wedding, her honored husband could testify that age had done nothing, to the last, to weaken the fervor—nay, hardly to diminish the romance of the union which had been blessed with unbroken peace, with uninterrupted confidence, with steady delight in each other's companionship; and what an inheritance do not her surviving children possess in the memory of such a devoted, faithful, and exemplary mother!

"Nor was this sweetness and goodness the fruit of constitutional amiability merely. Without that, indeed, her character could not have been what it was; but without something besides, it would certainly have lacked the wisdom and judgment, the prudence and self-restraint that marked her beneficence. She was no careless and sentimental almoner, hushing the sensitiveness of her own aching pity by ministering indiscriminately to the cries of idleness, imposture, and vice. She had known too well herself the discipline of honest toil, the uses of a self-denying economy, not to feel a strong disapprobation for sloth and self-indulgence. Nor was poverty in her experience such an unmitigated misfortune as to be treated with hasty and demoralizing largesses. She set no such valuation upon superfluity and luxury as to pity excessively those who taxed them. Her charities, constant and numerous, were painstaking, thoughtful, considerate. She gave as much counsel as money and as much time as means to this responsible office —one of the most serious and difficult of all Christian duties—the prudent, wise exercise of charity. If all the hearts here present could tell their own experience of her patient, wise, and prudent beneficence, it would fill these courts with the frankincense of honest gratitude and merited praise!

.   .   .   .

"You behold here no feeble relic of dainty idleness and unstrung fibres and soft and tended weakness. Here is what is left of a frame that has used every nerve and tissue in human service, household cares, diligent and painstaking duty to husband, children, and dependants. Here are the ashes of a woman of the Puritan and Huguenot spirit —one who knew nothing about the modern discontent with woman's sphere; nothing about the weariness of leisure and the lack of adequate occupation; nothing about the inequality of her woman's lot, or the monotony and oppression of a wife's and mother's duties. She found the place Providence gave her large enough for all her gifts, tasking and rewarding to all her efforts, and she did her full part in making, keeping, and spending her husband's fortune."

CONCLUSION.

Mr. Cooper's strong points of character are an impregnable sense of justice; an all-embracing philanthropy, and a keen instinct and wise discernment for the truth; especially in absolute and simple forms, such as it appears in the sayings of Christ, and in the maxims of the wise and good of all ages. He believes in these great truths with a simple heartiness and childlike fervor that makes it hard for him to realize at times that all men do not recognize them, or, if they do, they will not yield implicit obedience. They are no "glittering generalities" to him. He has faith in these simple maxims of wisdom and goodness, and he brings all institutions and methods of government to the test of their universal application. He is the most tolerant of men towards the frailties and shortcomings of individuals, but turns a stern face towards classes intrenched in privilege, and monopolies of all kinds. Without the discipline of the schools, without a systematic education, or special training of any kind derived from others, he has trained himself in the school of life to a large measure of practical and general knowledge, and acquired a specific skill, in a certain number of occupations during his long life, which could only be the result of great industry and devotion to his business occupations, sagacity in discerning their best conditions, and a marvellous facility in achieving success under difficulties, or of turning his course when success was not to be obtained any longer. His simple truthfulness makes him credulous, at times, in the honesty of some men who wish to deceive him; but he is never deceived long; and they rarely come off with any great advantage gained at his expense. With great energy, industry, economy, and a certain strictness in bargaining, which belongs to all acquisitive and accumulative natures, he has acquired a large fortune; but, outside of business, Mr. Cooper is as approachable, simple, and gentle as a child. He is open-handed to the poor and the destitute, melted by every tale of sorrow that is preferred to his ear; and lets thousands slip from his bountiful hand without a thought but of the good he designs. His character is based on sturdy honesty, impregnable justice, and common sense, with a something besides—a wonderful and rare nature that lies behind all his ordinary practical life among men, made up of ideal thoughts, inexpressible sympathies, and a great yearning for the morally good and the beautiful, that leads him sometimes into high regions of speculation, where practical men think that they cannot follow. But whoever studies these speculations of Mr. Cooper for the welfare of the race, or of his country, will see a germ of practical principles in them, a solid ground of wisdom on which they rest; so that if he had opportunities and adequate means to realize them, such as fall into the hands of the rulers of nations, he would turn his speculations into facts in the life of the nation. His ingenuity and his practical invention have been proved time and again; but he has also a certain speculative idealism in invention that has sometimes outrun his means and his practical ability to realize; but never without a sound principle at the bottom of his invention, which needed only more fortunate and favorable conditions than he could command.

Mr. Cooper is so broad, sincere, and catholic in his religious principles, that, I believe, he would be recognized by any minister of the Christian religion as a truly religious man; but his ecclesiasticism ends with a simple respect for all churches.

Mr. Cooper has all his life been devoted to business, but from an early period he has taken a personal interest and an active part in all the educational, social, and industrial progress of his native city, and often contributed in money and personal effort, very valuable services. He is by nature and temperament a radical reformer, but abhors destructiveness; so that he always looks to building up, before he thinks of pulling down. He respects vested rights and legal forms, even when he thinks they are opposed to the general welfare; and he will not consent to have them abolished without compensation to the losers.

The "crowning glory" of Mr. Cooper's life, and that on which he has expended the most money, time, and thought, is the "Cooper Union," commonly called the "Cooper Institute."

The corner-stone of this institution was laid twenty-one years ago, at the junction of Third and Fourth avenues, and their crossing with Eighth street. The original cost of the building was $634,000. It is in the centre of the industrial and trading population of New York, who are thus placed within easy reach of facilities chiefly designed for them. The institution consists of a series of free schools of instruction in practical art and science, a free reading-room, and free courses of popular lectures on subjects of science, art, and social reform. About twenty professors and instructors are employed and over fifty thousand dollars a year expended.

He is especially strenuous for a civil reform, and a "civil service" that shall secure to the country a qualified, honest, and permanent set of civil officers, educated to their special duties as are our military and naval officers. They should be examined and appointed by competent and permanent commissioners in every State, elected, or appointed irrespective of their politics. Politics should be confined to the electoral offices of the General Government, as they shape what is called the "policy of the Government." These civil officers, when they have worn out their powers in the service of the Government, he thinks should be pensioned, as are the military and naval officers.

These are the principles which Mr. Cooper sincerely entertains and has striven to realize all his life. Whether they are worthy the suffrages of the American people, let the people themselves judge. Mr. Cooper has never sought office, the office has sought him. Mr. Cooper is now in his eighty-seventh year, but hale and hearty beyond his years. He is especially young in that "youth of the heart" which gives the "verdure ever fresh" to life. Simple and pure in all his living, regular in his habits, active all the day, a sound sleeper at night, a man that lives much in "gentle mirth," he bids fair to live much beyond the term of ordinary life. He loves "the world," but hates the "flesh and the Devil." With a plain exterior, and without what is called "culture," he is every way a *true gentleman*—affable to his friends, kind to his dependants, full of respect and regard for woman, tender towards children, generous and sympathetic for the poor and the suffering, denying himself, and princely in his gifts to the world.

Mr. Cooper has written, or caused to be written under his supervision, a number of letters and pamphlets, the design of which has been to throw light upon the political questions of the day. They breathe his spirit and thought throughout, though not always in his own form of expression. Mr. Cooper has never been educated to composition as an art, nor is he familiar with those rhetorical forms of expression that grapple with difficult and abstract subjects, and give them thorough development and statement. His style is conversational and simple, and deals only with the simplest but grandest form of thought, where logic is at no account, and rhetoric of little avail. Hence, he has often intrusted to others the expression of his thought, for purposes of *discussing* a subject, and presenting it in proper form. But he always reads, carefully and conscientiously, whatever he causes to be written, and allows nothing to go forth to the public that is not properly and *substantially* the product of his own mind and the dictate of his best judgment.

In the following letters and public addresses of Mr. Cooper, we have his most carefully considered opinions and his own real sentiments, carefully written under his constant supervision and revision.

EDITOR.

New York, Sept. 1st, 1877.

NOMINATION TO THE PRESIDENCY
OF
PETER COOPER,
AND HIS
ADDRESS TO THE INDIANAPOLIS CONVENTION
OF THE
NATIONAL INDEPENDENT PARTY.

INTRODUCTION.

MR. COOPER's political ideas are very simple, and consist of two fundamental principles and their application to national life and happiness.

First, the *independence of a nation* must be secured from all foreign dictation, interference, or *even undue influence*, in its political and civil life, and in its *industrial business* and *financial* interests.

Secondly, in domestic administration, "*equal rights to all*" should prevail—*political, social*, and *industrial*—as necessary to the "preservation of life, liberty, and the pursuit of happiness."

These two fundamental principles, he thinks, are far from having been achieved in the history of nations.

The struggle for national life and happiness, now going on, consists in the vindication and practical application of the two principles of foreign independence and domestic rights. "Peace on earth and goodwill towards men" can only be obtained when nations cease to war on each other, *in any way*, and communities recognize and enforce equal rights for individuals. But Mr. Cooper recognizes the fact that, although nations may not be actually at war with each other, at some times, there is a *quasi* war, a state of hostility of "interests, but ill understood," a commercial and financial war going on, all the time, between nations.

The same is the fact in the domestic history of nations. Actual rebellions and revolutions result from a policy of hostility between the different classes that may divide the nation; but if these are not in progress, there is still going on, all the time, a *quasi* war of "interests but ill understood," between individuals and classes, that results in monopolies and unequal rights of all kinds.

To protect the people from this silent and selfish aggression of foreign influence, Mr. Cooper believes in a protective tariff, and a domestic currency incapable of exportation.

He believes that a tariff is really a tax on the foreign manufacturer and importer, and not on the *domestic buyer*, as it is usually represented by the sophistical argument of free trade. So far from making goods dearer than they could otherwise be, the competitions of foreign trade and the necessities of *selling somewhere*, make the foreign importer and manufacturer submit to the tariff, as a tax on their goods, while the practical result is an enhanced price, relatively, of all domestic manufactures and native products that are exchanged for the foreign goods. Any one may convince himself, by inquiring from domestic dealers in foreign goods, that the prices they have to give to the foreigner are rarely increased by a tariff on the importation; hence, the price is not increased to the consumer. All the complaints on the subject of tariff come from the foreign manufacturer and the large importing merchants, and from those who do not 'understand the true working of a tariff. The tariff is a premium to the domestic manufacturer, but no additional tax on the consumer, who from the very start buys his goods just as cheap from the foreigner, and in the long run a great deal cheaper from the domestic manufacturer. Mr. Cooper believes that the nearer the consumer is to the producer, the better for both; that the *greatest diversity of production* is the indispensable condition of the highest prosperity, independence, and the intellectual and moral advancement of any people. For this purpose, a "judicious tariff for revenue and protection" is absolutely necessary. It taxes the foreigner only; it encourages and diversifies our own domestic labor, and puts a premium on it, and frees the whole nation from the dependence upon and consequent tyranny of foreign nations.

For the same object of commercial protection, Mr. Cooper desires a purely domestic currency, unexportable as merchandise, like gold and silver, and incapable of interference by the demands and exactions of foreign trade. Every nation ought to have such a domestic currency, and keep it "on a par" with the currency of all other nations, by the reciprocities and "equal balances" of their mutual exchanges in each other's products and manufactures. It is axiomatic that *the money of a creditor nation will always be* "*above par*" *with that of a debtor nation.* If, therefore, the money of a debtor nation can be exported, as gold and silver, it will flow out to the creditor nation, and leave the debtor in distress and business embarrassment, till its money can be drawn back by sacrifices of domestic goods and products. This exportable currency gives a "fatal facility" of getting in debt with foreign nations. Instead of paying with goods and products, our only proper resource, we pay with *our money*, which we cannot spare from our own domestic trade and the payment of labor. The periodical "panics" have always resulted from a "drain of specie," when that was our only legal tender. No device or enactment of Government can prevent this; because it cannot control the price of money, when money is also merchandise all over the world, as is also gold and silver. Hence the Government cannot protect the people from periodic disaster and distress to the domestic trade, and the stoppage of the bread of the poor; from the extravagance of the rich of our own nation, in foreign goods, and the insidious temptations to trade in the cheap labor of other nations. To make our domestic currency on a par with gold or silver, or any foreign currency, Mr. Cooper thinks, our Government should make it of the most indispensable use as legal tender for all debts and Government dues; fix its price, equitably, by the interest paid on it, when converted into bonds, prevent over-issues by strict and just regulations as to the issue of bonds or currency, and let the people themselves always regulate the relative amount of each, by the "interconvertible bond."

The tariff and the "domestic currency," are the two great means of defence which Mr. Cooper sets up against the "war of commerce," which all nations are now urging against each other, amidst the reciprocities, the fair exchanges, and the civilizing intercourse which a true commerce and trade engender among nations.

He has no objection to gold and silver coin being also a "legal tender," as well as paper. It is so in France. The objection that "it will set up three standards for the payment of debts," and the injustice to the creditor by the fluctuations in value of either standard, is more than met by the fact that gold and silver, as the present money of the world, do not fluctuate much, except as the currents of the world's commerce ebb and flow; and this cannot be controlled by Government, but must be guarded against by a domestic paper currency, from leaving us with too little money at any time to do business with; while the paper can be made of stable value by proper Government regulation and the "interconvertible bond." Making gold and silver coin a legal tender will tend to enhance their value among us, encourage the production of gold and silver, in which the country is very rich, and equalize our exchanges with foreign nations more, by furnishing them what they now desire the most, in exchange for their commodities.*

So far from giving occasion and instruments to the selfishness, or greed, or love of power of individuals and classes, Government is espe-

---

* Mr. Cooper thinks now that the Government paper should be the *exclusive* legal tender; and by keeping its volume at a certain fixed ratio, per capita, receivable for all taxes and duties, and made *interconvertible* with Government bonds, the paper could be kept *on a par* with the standard dollar of gold or silver.

cially constituted to keep an even balance among the rights of the people, and not only protect their lives and property from the violence that springs from such passions, but from the cunning devices of law and vested privileges by which the few, often take away the rights of the many, or even the banding together, under cunning forms and pretences, of some one class,—politicians, bondholders, importers, bankers, or "syndicates and rings" of all kinds, to defraud and deceive the people. This is indeed a difficult task. This is the silent war going on at all times in a nation, which brings on, sooner or later, revolutions and rebellions, unless the differences can be allayed by reason, justice, and humanity, embodied in law, and faithfully administered by Government. This ought to be the proper object of all "parties" and administrations. But late events have shown that, while our form of Government is the best in the world, it is, in some respects, the worst administered. The rapid growth in wealth and the wonderful material resources that tempt the cupidity of this people, have got in advance of their moral and intellectual development, and engendered a venality and greed for wealth that has crept into the halls of legislation and into the courts of justice. Politics have become a trade for office, and the wealthy are turning their attention to politics, as means of monopoly and lucrative gain, greater than mere legitimate business alone can offer. This is indeed a sad sign of political decay and venal corruption in public affairs, of which official peculations, such as the Tweeds and the Belknaps engage in, are the mere outcrops of what can be found deeper and more general under the surface. It is such convictions as these that are bringing honest men to the front, who else, like Mr. Cooper, would shrink from observation, and prefer private life to all the honors of public office. There is a sense of real danger pervading the honorable and good minds of this country, that our republic cannot last much longer if "this order of things" is allowed to go on; that "something must be done to change the men and measures that now control public affairs, or we shall end in revolution and despotism." What complicates the difficulty is, that under this very cry of reform, bad men are trying to get control of public affairs, from the free suffrages of the people. If the people cannot discriminate, or allow themselves to be deceived in this crisis of the nation's history, we must follow the precedent of other nations, under similar circumstances, and lose our liberties from similar causes.

Mr. Cooper's mind has been so strongly impressed with this state of things, that at an advanced age, when he would gladly seek repose, but with a life of honorable toil and honest record behind him, never having sought office or political preferment in his life, he consented, at the earnest solicitation of friends, to accept the nomination as chief magistrate of this nation in the spring of 1876. This is itself one of the signs of reaction in the people's mind against the ruling class. The people are suffering, and they have no hopes of amelioration from those who ask to administer the Government, but a continuance of the policy of administration to which they owe their sufferings. Mr. Cooper thinks this is "cruel and unjust." He demands an entire change in two particulars: First, in the financial policy of the government; Secondly, in an organized "civil reform," both in the appointment and election to office, that shall secure the best and most competent men to rule and to serve this people.

He thinks that "politicians" may have a place, and have a very useful function in the "body politic;" but they must not be allowed to control the appointment of all the civil offices in the gift of the Government, and make them the "chess-men" in their game of public life, and the means of keeping themselves in power.

Mr. Cooper also thoroughly believes in the *paternal character and functions* of every Republican Government. The general Government, in its sphere, and the local Governments, in their several spheres, in the States and municipalities, should have a *paternal spirit* and oversight towards the mass of the people. The poor and the maimed, the pauper and the criminal, the unfortunate and the suffering who have no private relief or help, should be looked after and cared for by the local and municipal Governments. He believes that public improvements and works of a national character are proper objects of the general Government; and the encouragement of immigration and the settlement of the public lands are the proper objects of care and special provision by the Government. On a large scale, the honest and industrious poor of our own people and those of other nations, can be provided for, the country enriched, and made the true home and paradise of freedom for the laboring man. All these ideas and opinions Mr. Cooper has enlarged and dwelt upon in the following writings and publications, which he has given to the country for the last twenty years, and especially since the war of the rebellion; and the changes and difficulties of that war, which have called to the front the best councillors of the nation.

THE NOMINATION OF MR. COOPER.

On the 17th of May, 1876, a large and enthusiastic convention of the friends of a specific national currency, commonly called the "Greenback," met, and organized the "National Independent Party."

The convention adopted a platform, and nominated unanimously Mr Peter Cooper as their candidate for the Presidency of the United States.

Mr. Cooper was telegraphed the result, but peremptorily declined, at first, for personal reasons. Afterwards, on the earnest representations of friends, he made a *conditional* acceptance, based upon the hope that one of the subsequent conventions to be held by both the Republican and Democratic parties might assume a favorable aspect towards the financial doctrines of the Independent party. In this hope he was entirely disappointed, as well as in the two letters of acceptance of the two candidates nominated by their respective parties. Mr. Cooper then addressed an "open letter" to those candidates and to the country, accepting, finally, and unconditionally, his nomination, and giving his reasons for the same.

We give here, first, his address to the convention of the Independent party.

Secondly, the platform adopted by the convention.

Thirdly, Mr. Cooper's letter of *conditional* acceptance.

Fourthly, the "open letter" of final acceptance.

MR. PETER COOPER'S ADDRESS

" *To the Convention, held at Indianapolis, of the National Independent Party, May 17th, 1876.*

" Gentlemen of the Convention :

" We have met, my friends, to unite in a course of efforts to find out, and, *if possible*, to remove a cause of evil that has shrunk the value of the real estate of the nation to a condition where it cannot be sold, or mortgages obtained on it for much more than one-half the amount that the same property would have brought three years ago. This dire calamity has been brought on our country by the acts of our Government. The first act took from the national money its power to pay interest on bonds and duties on imports. The second act has contracted the currency of the country until it has shrunk the value of property to its present condition by destroying public confidence ; and that without shrinking any of the debts contracted in its use.

" I do most humbly hope that I shall be able to show the fatal causes that have been allowed to operate and bring this wretchedness and ruin to the homes of untold thousands of the men and the women throughout our country.

" Facts will show that it was the unwise acts of our own Government that have allowed a policy to prevail, more in the interest of foreign governments than our own.

" It was these unwise acts of legislation that brought discredit on our national money, as I have said, by introducing into the law that created it that *terrible* word *except*, which took from our legal money its power to pay interest on bonds, and duties on imports.

" The introduction of that little word *except* into the original law *drew tears from the eyes* of Thaddeus Stephens when he looked down the current of events and saw our bonds in the hands of foreigners, who would be receiving a gold interest on every hundred dollars of bonds that cost them but fifty or sixty dollars in gold.

" *But* for the introduction of that word *except* into that original law, our bonds would have been taken at par by our own people, and the interest would have been paid at home in currency, instead of being paid to foreigners in gold.

" An additional calamity has been brought on our country by a national policy that has taken from the people their *currency, the tools of their trades,* the very life-blood of the traffic and commerce of our country.

" Facts show that in 1865 there was in the hands of the people, as a currency, $58 per head, and that at a time of our greatest national prosperity.

" We have now arrived at a time of unequalled adversity, with a currency in 1875 of 17\frac{33}{100}$ per capita, with failures amounting to two hundred millions of dollars in a year.

" Among the causes that now afflict the country, it may be well to *look* at the enormous increase in our foreign importations, which amounted to 359 millions in the year 1868, and increased to 684 millions of dollars in 1873, and was 574 millions of dollars in 1875.

" I think you will agree with me, when I say that prosperity can never be restored to our beloved country by a national policy that enforces idleness and financial distress on so vast a number of the laborers and business men of this country. Our nation's wealth must forever depend on the application of knowledge, economy, and well-directed labor to all the useful and necessary purposes of life, but also a proper legislation for the people.

" The American people can never buy anything cheap from foreign countries that must be bought at the cost of leaving our own good raw materials unused, and our own labor unemployed.

" I find myself compelled to believe that much of the past legislation of our country, in reference to tariff and currency, has been adopted under the advice and influence of men in the interest of foreign nations that have a direct motive to mislead and deceive us. Our prosperity as a nation will commence to return when the Congress of our country shall assume its own inherent sovereign right to furnish all the inhabitants of the United States a redeemable, uniform, unfluctuating national currency.

"I do heartily agree with Senator Jones, when he says that 'the present is the acceptable time to undo the unwitting and blundering work of 1873; and to render our legislation on the subject of money, consistent with the physical facts, concerning the stock and supply of the precious metals throughout the world, and conformable to the constitution of our country.'

"I sincerely hope that the concluding advice of Senator Jones will make a living and lasting impression, when he says, speaking to the present Senate, 'We cannot, we dare not, avoid speedy action on the subject. Not only does reason, justice, and authority unite in urging us to retrace our steps, but the organic law commands us to do so; and the presence of peril enjoins what the law commands.'

"The Senator states a most important fact, and one that all know to be true, 'that by interfering with the standards of the country, Congress has led the country away from the realms of prosperity, and thrust it beyond the bounds of safety.' He says, truly, 'to refuse to replace it upon its former vantage ground would be to incur a responsibility and a deserved reproach, greater than that which men have ever before felt themselves able to bear.'

"It will require all the wisdom that can be gathered from the history and experience of the past to enable us to work out our salvation from the evils that an unwise legislation has brought on our country.

"It will be found that nothing short of a full, fair, and frank performance of the first duty enjoined on Congress by the Constitution will ever restore permanent prosperity to us as a nation.

.   .   .   .

"It is a remarkable fact that the most essential element of our colonial and national prosperity was obtained by the use of the legal-tender paper money—the very thing that our present rulers seem now determined to hold up to ridicule and contempt. We are apt to forget that the 'continental money' secured for us a country, and the 'greenback' currency has saved us as a nation.

"Sir A. Alison, the able and indefatigable English historian, has borne testimony to the superior power and value of paper money. He says: 'When sixteen hundred thousand men, on both sides, were in the continental wars with France in Germany and Spain alone, where nothing could be purchased except by specie, it is not surprising that guineas went where they were so much needed, and bore so high a price.' . . . 'In truth such was the need of precious metals, owing to this cause, that one-tenth of the currency of the world was attracted to Germany as a common centre, and the demand could not be supplied; and by a decree in September, 1813, from Peterwalsden, in Germany, the allied sovereigns issued paper notes, guaranteed by Russia, Prussia, and England. These notes passed as cash from Kamskatkha to the Rhine, and gave the currency which brought the war to a successful close.'

" In a recent edition of the 'History of Europe,' Sir A. Alison gives an additional evidence of the important advantages which experience has demonstrated to result from the use of paper currency.

" He says, 'To the suspension of cash payments by the act of 1797, and the power in consequence vested in the Bank of England, of expanding its paper circulation in proportion to the abstraction of a metallic currency, the wants of the country and the resting of the national industry on a basis not liable to be taken away by the mutations of commerce or the necessities of war—it is to these facts that the salvation of the empire must be ascribed.' . . . 'It is remarkable that this admirable system, which may be truly called the working power of nations during war, became at the close of the war the object of the most determined hostility on the part of the great capitalists and chief writers of Political Economy in the country.' . . . 'Here, however,' says Alison, 'as everywhere else, experience, the great test of the truth, has determined the question. The adoption of the opposite system of contracting the paper currency in proportion to the abstraction of the metallic currency by the acts of 1819 and 1844, followed as they were by the monetary crises of 1825, 1839, and 1847, have demonstrated beyond a doubt that it was in the system of an expansive currency that Great Britain, during the war, found the sole means of her salvation. From 1797 to 1815 commerce, manufactures, and agriculture advanced in England, in spite of all the evils of war, with a rapidity greater than they had previously done in centuries before. This proves beyond a doubt the power of paper money to increase the wealth of a nation.'

" It is worth while to observe that this same Sir A. Alison, who speaks so wisely on this subject in reference to the history of his own country, while scanning a few years ago the prosperity of our country during the war of the Rebellion and immediately after, has a foreboding of what might happen, and remarks: 'The American Government may make financial and legislative mistakes which may check the progress of the nation and counteract the advantages which paper money has already bestowed upon them; they may adopt the unwise and unjust system which England adopted at the close of the French war; they may resolve to pay in gold, and with low prices, the debt contracted with paper, and with high prices. But whatever they may do,' he adds, ' nothing can shake the evidence which the experience of that nation during the last six years affords of the power of paper money to promote a nation's welfare.'

" Sir Walter Scott, in his ' Malachi Margrowther's Letters,' shows how the wealth of a nation is increased by paper money. ' I assume,' he says, ' without hazard of contradiction, that banks have existed in Scotland for near one hundred and twenty years ; that they have flourished, and the country has flourished with them ; and that during the last twenty years particularly the notes, and especially the small notes which the banks distribute, supply all the demand for a medium of currency. This system has so completely expelled gold from Scotland that you never by any chance espy a guinea there, except in the purse of an accidental stranger, or in the coffers of the banks themselves. But the facilities which this paper has afforded to the industrious and enterprising agriculturists and manufacturers, as well as to the trustees of the public, in executing national works, have converted Scotland from a poor, miserable, barren country into one where, if nature has done less, art and industry have done more than, perhaps, in any other country in Europe, England not excepted.'

" President Grant, in his message of 1873, said, ' The experience of the present panic has proven that the currency of the country, based, as it is, upon its credit, is the best that has ever been devised.' . . . ' In view of the great actual contraction that has taken place in the currency, and the comparative contraction continuously going on, due to the increase of the population, the increase of manufactories and of all industries, I do not believe there is too much of it now for the dullest period of the year.'

" Notwithstanding these recommendations of the President, Congress has continued to tax the people and contract the national currency in a vain effort to arrive at specie payments.

" Our Government should have left that amount of currency in the hands of the people, which the necessities of war had compelled it to put in circulation as the only means of the national salvation.

" Every dollar of currency paid out, whether gold, silver, or paper, was given out for ' value received,' and thus became, by the act of the Government, a valid claim for a dollar's worth of the whole property of the country. Hence, not a dollar of it should ever have been withdrawn.

"It is now almost universally believed that had the Treasury notes continued, as at first issued, to be received for all forms of taxes, duties, and debts, they would have circulated to this day, as they did then, as so much gold, precisely as the Government paper did circulate in France when put upon the same footing.

"This would have saved our country more than one-half of the amount of the whole expenses of the war in the present shrinkage of values and the interruption to honest industry. It would have saved us, also, from the perpetual drainage of gold to pay interest on our foreign indebtedness.

"Gentlemen of the Convention, I have heretofore enlarged upon what seemed to me the true financial policy of this country in pamphlets and writings that I have had the honor to lay before the country, so that it would be a vain repetition to go much into that subject now.

"The paper currency, commonly called 'legal tenders' or 'greenbacks,' was actually paid out for value received as so much gold, when gold could not be obtained.

"This being an incontrovertible fact, it follows that every Treasury note, demand note, or legal tender, given out as money, in payment for any form of labor and property received by the Government, became, in the possession of its owners, real dollars that could not be taken constitutionally from the people, except by uniform taxes, as on other property.

"But whether our currency will be always on a par with gold or not, I have shown from history, and incontrovertible facts prove it, that the commercial and industrial prosperity of a country do not depend upon the amount of gold and silver there is in circulation. Our prosperity must continually depend upon the industry, the enterprise, and the busy internal trade and a true independence of foreign nations, which a paper circulation, well based on sound credit, has always been found to promote.

"But I believe prosperity can never again bless our glorious country until justice is established, by giving back to the people the exact amount of currency found in circulation at the close of the war. That was the price of the nation's life. It ought to be restored and made the permanent and unfluctuating measure of all values, through all coming time—never to be increased or diminished, only, as per capita, with the increase of the inhabitants of our country.

"This currency must be made receivable for all forms of taxes, duties, ana debts, and convertible into interest-bearing bonds, at some equitable rate of interest, and reconvertible into currency at the will of the holder. This, we believe, will secure uniformity of value to a degree that gold has never attained. President Steele, of Lawrence University, has well said on this subject:

"'In fixing a standard, it is essential to select something that is as nearly as possible invariable. The conventional unit of lineal measure must not be a line which averages a foot, though it may be fourteen inches to-day and nine inches to-morrow. The bushel measure should not contain two or three quarts more or less at one time than at another. 'For the same reason it is desirable that the unit of *value* should have the same purchasing power next week that it has now.'

"In conclusion, Gentlemen, I think we have reason to congratulate ourselves on the great awakening of the public mind in regard to this question of finance. The people are beginning to recognize their rights and their duties in this matter. I think the time has come to exhort every one to go to the ballot-box and select good and true men, who will legislate in accordance with justice, the Constitution, and the true interests of the people; and give us what will always stand as a monument of political wisdom, a true national currency.

" With devout wishes for the success of all measures tending to this object, I remain yours, in the common interests of our beloved country."

THE PLATFORM OF THE INDEPENDENT PARTY.

The following is the Platform of the Independent Party, as adopted by its National Convention at Indianapolis:

" The Independent Party is called into existence by the necessities of the people whose industries are prostrated, whose labor is deprived of its just reward as the result of the serious mismanagement of the national finances, which errors both the Republican and Democratic parties neglect to correct. In view of the failure of these parties to furnish relief to the depressed industries of the country, thereby disappointing the just hopes and expectations of a suffering people, we declare our principles and invite all independent and patriotic men to join our ranks in this movement for financial reform and industrial emancipation.

" First—We demand the immediate and unconditional repeal of the Specie-resumption Act of January 14, 1875, and the rescue of our industries from the disaster and ruin resulting from its enforcement, and we call upon all patriotic men to organize in every Congressional district of the country, with the view of electing representatives in Congress who will legisate for, and a Chief Magistrate who will carry out the wishes of, the people in this regard, and thus stop the present suicidal and destructive policy of contraction.

"Second—We believe that United States notes, issued directly by the Government and convertible on demand into United States obligations, bearing an equitable rate of interest (not exceeding one cent a day on each one hundred dollars), and interchangeable with United States notes at par, will afford the best circulating medium ever devised; such United States notes should be a full legal tender for all purposes, except for the payment of such obligations as are by existing contracts expressly made payable in coin. And we hold that it is the duty of the Government to provide such a circulating medium, and we insist, in the language of Thoman Jefferson, 'that bank paper must be suppressed and the circulation restored to the nation, to whom it belongs.'

"Third—It is the paramount duty of the Government in all its legislation to keep in view the full development of all legitimate business, agricultural, mining, manufacturing, and commercial.

"Fourth—We most earnestly protest against any further issue of gold bonds, for sale in foreign markets, by means of which we would be made, for a longer period, hewers of wood and drawers of water for foreign nations, especially as the American people would gladly and promptly take at par all the bonds the Government may need to sell, provided they are made payable at the option of the holder, although bearing interest at three and sixty-five one-hundredths per cent. per annum, or even a lower rate.

"Fifth—We further protest against the sale of Government bonds for the purpose of buying silver to be used as a substitute for our more convenient and less fluctuating fractional currency, which, although well calculated to enrich the owners of silver mines, yet in operation will still further oppress through taxation an already overburdened people."

MR. COOPER'S ACCEPTANCE.

"NEW YORK, May 31, 1876.

"Hon. MOSES W. FIELD, Chairman, and Hon. THOMAS J. DURANT, Secretary of the National Executive Council of the Independent Party:

"GENTLEMEN—Your formal, official notification of the unanimous nomination, tendered by the National Convention of the Independent Party at Indianapolis, on the 17th instant, to me for the high office of President of the United States is before me; . . . together with an authenticated copy of the admirable platform which the Convention adopted.

5

" While I most heartily thank the Convention through you for the great honor they have thus conferred upon me, kindly permit me to say that there is a bare possibility, if wise counsels prevail, that the sorely-needed relief from the blighting effects of past unwise legislation relative to finance, which the people so earnestly seek, may yet be had through either the Republican or Democratic party; both of them meeting in national convention at an early date.

" It is unnecessary for me to assure you that while I have no aspiration for the position of Chief Magistrate of this great Republic, I will most cheerfully do what I can to forward the best interests of my country.

" I, therefore, accept your nomination, *conditionally*, expressing the earnest hope that the Independent Party may yet attain its exalted aims, while permitting me to step aside and remain in that quiet which is most congenial to my nature and time of life.

" Most respectfully yours,

" Peter Cooper."

AN OPEN LETTER BY PETER COOPER TO THE CANDIDATES FOR THE PRESIDENCY, NOMINATED BY THE REPUBLICAN AND DEMOCRATIC PAR-TIES, IN CONVENTION ASSEMBLED.

" New York, July 25th, 1876.

" *Hon. R. B. Hayes and Hon. Samuel J. Tilden.*

" Gentlemen :—

" I find myself impelled by an irresistible anxiety for my country; by the palpable facts of distress and suffering that surround me, and which I am compelled to know pervade the families of the great mass of our people; by the earnest calls that have been made to me from all parts of this great country; and especially by the solemn and deliberate act of an earnest and intelligent body of my fellow-citizens, in convention assembled, who, setting forth clearly their convictions as to the real cause of this wide-spread distress among the masses of our countrymen, have called upon me to represent those convictions, and nominated me as their chief executive to carry them out;—by all these considerations I feel called upon to address a few words to you, who now hold the nominations of the two great organized political parties in this country for the highest positions of responsibility as to the future happiness and prosperity of this great people.

" Far be it from me to attribute any want of patriotism or any unworthy motive to your honorable selves, or to the leaders of those conventions which have nominated you both, respectively, to the high office of the President of the United States. But the imminent question of the day, that which touches the cause of the present financial ruin and suffering of so many, is one of such palpable facts and simple deductions therefrom, that I must think there is some mistake in the radical principle by which these facts are viewed by you and the great parties which you represent. I find in the platforms of the conventions of the two great parties no adequate expression either of the facts, the causes, or the principles that underlie the present great distress of our nation, when thousands of honest, industrious people are filled with anxiety for the bread of their families, or are suffering already from an inadequate supply. This seems to me the great and paramount question of the day, to which our chief thought and most efficient action should be directed, and before which all other questions should sink into insignificance.

" What is the cause of this wide-spread ruin and present distress, and what is the immediate remedy ?

" A few facts of history and of public record will show this. According to Spaulding's Financial History of the War (p. 201) the public debt of the United States stood on the books of the Treasury, October 1st, 1865, at a total of $2,803,549,437. According to the same author, who is a strong advocate for specie payments (page 10, Introduction), out of this debt, in 1864, ' the inflating paper issues, outstanding, were over $1,100,000,000,'—and gold reached its highest quotation, 2.85.

" Now, be it remembered, that although a few money-changers, speculators, and importers were willing to give $2.85 of paper for one dollar in gold, yet the people were using this paper to buy flour and exchange their commodities at prices that were far less than this inflated price of gold.

" Gold was no longer the standard of exchange except in foreign commodities where 'balances' had to be paid in gold. The internal trade, commerce, and industries of the country were steadily increasing, and never before so flourishing as during the time of this famine for gold. In an evil hour, it became the policy of this Government to reduce all our paper currency to the standard and par value of gold. This was attempted by the withdrawal of the paper currency as fast as practicable, and by absorbing the same by an arbitrary law, into a debt for so much gold as the face of the paper, in the shape of gold bonds, bearing the yearly interest of six per cent. in gold ! In the course of less than eight years this change was effected, and the people's money and currency of all kinds were reduced subsequently from $2,192,395,527, as represented on the Treasurer's books on September 1, 1865, to the sum of $631,488,676 on the 1st of November, 1873, making a reduction of the currency in eight years of $1,561,906,851 ! (See Congressional Record, March 31, 1874, speech of John M. Bright, of Tennessee.) This brought on the panic of 1873 and all our present financial troubles. Although a part of this vast sum was a kind of currency that drew interest, and, therefore, partook also of the nature of an investment, yet, as Mr. Maynard, Chairman of the Committee on Banking and Currency, said, from his seat in Congress, on occasion of Mr. Bright's speech, ' those issues were engraved and prepared in a form to circulate as money, and, as a matter of fact, did so circulate,' until either they were funded or ' the interest accumulated so as to make them superior to the ordinary class of currency.' But this stupendous decrease in the people's money—the very tools of their trades and enterprises of every description, the use of which they had fairly earned by the blood and sacrifices of a great war, and the beneficial effects of which were proved by the great activity in business and trade which it engendered as long as it lasted—this great reduction in the money of the people was made by methods equally unjust, as they were disastrous to the prosperity of the country.

"This paper currency was absorbed by interest-bearing gold bonds, which were bought by the paper, which in its turn had been purchased by gold at 40, 50, and 60 per cent. discount; thus turning the debt of the country to one of twice its value in paper, and paying for the gold bonds at half their value in paper. This was done at a time when this paper currency was doing the nation all the good that so much gold could do for our domestic prosperity and trade. The people were building up the country with a rapidity unexampled before, with this paper, which, if it had been fully honored by the Government that issued it, and received for all imports, duties, and debts, and allowed to be exchanged at par for bonds at an equitable rate of interest, would not have permitted any premium on gold.

" These are the facts. The panic of '73 and all the consequent distress of the industrial classes of our country, and its baffled enterprise, is distinctly due to the contraction of the currency to this enormous extent during the eight years preceding 1873. It stopped credit, production, and consumption, and made much of what currency was left rush, in a panic, to the head money-centres—as the blood in an apoplectic fit rushes to the head—where this money is now vainly seeking investment, ' in first-class security,' at two per cent.; while the country at large is palsied in its enterprises and industries for want of this very currency. And what was all this done for? To change the debt of the country without reducing its real amount, from a shape beneficial to the people, and incorporated as an integral part of the very life-blood of all their rising industries and their growing trade—this paper currency was turned, almost with the suddenness of a conjuration, and by the forms of an arbitrary construction of law, into another shape, twice in amount as measured by the same paper, and taxing the people interest on it, in gold, to the amount of $94,684,269 per year. (See statement of the public debt, June, 1876.)

" Most of this interest is now paid to foreign bondholders, alien to our institutions and uninterested in our prosperity, except to keep up our ability and willingness to bear taxation.

"And what is the specious reason for this change? ' *To return to specie payments !* '

" What can this policy result in but a further distress and impoverishment of this people and the building up of the interests of a class whose business it is to invest or to lend money, and whose policy will be to get the highest rate of interest? Such are apt to forget that the immediate gain of such a policy is far less than that which arises from the prosperity of the whole people, and the multiplication of wealth that comes from enterprise unimpeded and industry constantly employed. We may concede all that is claimed of the necessity of ' specie payments,' and our currency being made on a par with gold. But this disastrous and ill-judged method of reaching specie payments, by the past and present contraction of our currency, is very unjust and cruel to our people ; for it shrunk the value of all property, so that it could not be sold, or mortgages obtained on it, for more than one-half the amount that the same property would have brought three years previous, and reduced the wages of labor to the same degree. This return to 'specie payments' may be made without such injury, by honoring the currency in every way ; by making it exclusively the money as well as the legal tender of the country ; by receiving it for all forms of taxes, duties, debts to Government, as well as the payment of all private debts ; by establishing its value on a firm basis, at a fixed and equitable rate of interest, which it may always find in an interconvertible bond ; and by determining the volume of the currency, where the unobstructed laws of the internal trade and industry of this country may require it to be, under the free use of the interconvertible bond. This great national debt ought to be held as a great trust by the Government of this people, and made the receptacle of all the trust funds, and the savings of all the poor among our own people. It should be an investment put within the reach of our own people, instead of being sent abroad to swell the coffers of the rich in other countries.

"If the Government, after the war of rebellion, had been as anxious to heal the wounds which that unhappy war created, to alleviate the poverty which it brought on a large section of our country, to reinstate the broken industries and enterprises of our whole people, as it had been to carry that war vigorously, at any cost, on to victory, the Government would have seen that peace had its demands as well as war. If a Government is bound to protect the people from the aggressions of war, it is also bound to save it from commercial distress, and the sorrows of a laboring population without work. The Government might now free hundreds of thousands from imminent want, and set the wheels of trade again in motion by building the two great railroads across the Continent at the Southwest and Northwest of the country that private enterprise has already commenced, but cannot complete, for want of capital. The legal tender of a solvent country like this, cannot be called a *debt* in any proper sense of the word. *It is money*, and measures the exchangeable value of all property, gold included. All must see that the currency paid out by the Government for value received became the people's money, over which the Government lost all control, except to tax it, as all other property, to meet the wants of Government. This amount of money, even now, may be given back to the people in works of great national importance, like that of a Northern & Southern Pacific Railroad, that would, to-day, be worth their cost in aiding to put down the Indian wars that now threaten the frontier of our country. What is a Government good for, if in such a country as this, with all its material resources, and vast extent, it cannot prevent a large part of its people from the distress of want of work and of bread? This seems to me the first duty of Government.

"Sorry am I to see, and I say it without any reproach cast upon the integrity of those concerned, that in neither of the platforms of the political parties that represent the governing intelligence and wealth of this country is this great question of finance either discussed or recognized in its principles, or bearings upon the happiness and prosperity of this people—except in a way that seems to me adverse to both.

"I have, therefore, consented, with great reluctance, to go before the people—not for the strife of office, not for the petty triumphs of a successful candidate, but for the vindication of a great principle that underlies all true Republican or Democratic Institutions—namely, that the interest and happiness of the whole people are superior to the demands or interests of any one class; that in the neglect or defiance of this prin ciple, the great debt of this people, incurred by a war to save the life of this nation, has been administered too much by the advice and in the interest of a small class that care for their income, but cannot look out for, or attend to active investments; hence, they prefer the bond to the currency; and for another class who desire the highest interest for the smallest investment; hence they prefer gold to a paper legal tender; and for still another class who, alien to our institutions and country, care only to tax its energies and wealth for the highest interest they can draw for an immediate investment of their money. But these are not the interests of the people of this country. Neither honor nor justice requires such administration of the public debt of this country.

"I feel, therefore, constrained by every principle of honor and love for my country to come forward at an advanced age, and with a mind that would gladly seek repose, after the toils of a long and laborious life, to answer the call of a portion of my countrymen, to try these issues before the people of the whole country; to test these truths which we hold to be self-evident, as soon as they are honestly examined, as are the truths of the Declaration of Independence. One of the chief of these truths is that as all rightful Governments are made for the people and by the people; they must be administered with a parental care in the interests of the whole people, and not for a class. No single interest touches the domestic comfort and prosperity of the people as this one of the currency; and in the present condition of the country, none is of so much immediate importance or calls for more immediate solution. To put off this question, therefore, with vague expressions of reform, and the desirableness of 'specie payments,' is to ignore the ruling interest of the hour. It is to surrender the people to their sufferings without any promise of remedy.

"I appeal, therefore, from those who seem insensible to the cry of the people to the people themselves. I appeal from the political parties, organized to control the Government, and distribute the offices and emoluments of office, to the great industrial classes who are organized to protect their interests and obtain some recognition of their rights from the Government of the country. Let them substitute co-operation for 'strikes,' and unite to save themselves and the country from the present disaster and distress to all the industrial classes. Let no man think of the bullet while he has the ballot in his hand. It needs but the use of that simple instrument of political power to rectify all our discontents and social evils.

"Let us have our national currency duly honored; let us take the testimony of the nation's experience, and that of other countries, as to what such currency can do for our prosperity; let the gold par be reached by rendering our currency of higher and indispensable uses, as now exemplified in France, and not by contracting its amount; and let its volume and its value be determined by the interconvertible bond, placed at the disposal of the wants of the people and governed by all the forms and sanctities of law; and not surrender the currency to the ever-changing basis of a commodity like gold—and we shall have peace on this question. 'Justice will be established and the general welfare promoted;' prosperity again will revisit us, and we shall vindicate the wisdom and superiority of our free institutions before the world.

" France, with her 600,000,000 of legal paper, has kept her industries profitably employed by keeping her paper receivable for all forms of *taxes, duties, and debts.*

" My views upon the currency I have heretofore briefly expressed as follows :

" ' The worth or exchangeable value of gold is as uncertain as other products of human labor, such as wheat or cotton. The exchangeable value of anything depends on its *convertibility into something else* that has value *at the option of the individual.* This rule applies to paper money as to anything else. But how shall Government give an exchangeable value to a paper currency? Can it be done by a standard which is beyond its control and which naturally fluctuates, while the sign of exchange indicated by the paper remains the same?

" ' This is the unsound theory which possesses the minds of our people and of our politicians.

" ' We must cut loose from this unreasonable theory, or we shall be subject, for all time, to these periodic disturbances of our currency which bring such wide-spread ruin and distress to our commercial industries, and work, on the part of the Government, *positive and cruel injustice.* The remedy seems to me to be very plain.

" ' First—We must put this whole power of coining money or issuing currency, as Thomas Jefferson says, " where, by the Constitution, it properly belongs "—entirely into the hands of our Government. That Government is a Republic, hence it is under the control of the people. Corporations and States have hitherto, in some form or other, divided this power with the Government. Hence come the embarrassments and the fluctuations, as may be easily shown.

" ' But now we must trust our Government with this *whole function* of providing the standards and measures of exchange, as we trust it with the weights and measures of trade. So far from putting the people in the power of our Government and at the caprice of parties in power,

I contend it will bring the Government more under control of the people and give a check to mere party rule. For the more stake the people have in the wisdom and honesty of the Government, the more watchful and firm they will be in its control.

"'SECONDLY—We must require the Government to make this currency, at all times, and, at the option of the individual, *convertible*. But the currency must be convertible into something over which the Government has entire control, and to which it can give a definite as well as a permanent value. This is its own *interest-bearing bonds*. These are, in fact, a mortgage upon the embodied wealth of the whole country. The reality of their value is as sound and as permanent as the Government itself, and the degree of their value can be determined exactly by the rate of interest the Government may think proper to fix.'

"The time has come when the claims of a common humanity, and all that can move the manhood of an American citizen, must unite in a demand for an act of common justice now due to the American people who have saved our country from ruin, and will, I trust, forever protect it. The Constitution has made it the first and the most important duty of Congress ' to establish *justice, insure domestic tranquillity, provide for the common defence, promote the general welfare, and secure the blessings of liberty to ourselves and our posterity.*'

"To my personal friends I need not say that this sacrifice of peace and rest is like the surrender of what remnant of life I may have. But to the country at large, I will say that I am willing to stand in the place where I have been put by the judgment of an intelligent and honest portion of my countrymen, to stand with them, and try before the whole people this cause of the people's money, and the true financial policy of this Government.

" Most respectfully yours,

" PETER COOPER."

A LETTER ON THE CURRENCY.

By PETER COOPER.

ADDRESSED IN 1875.

To the Editors and Legislators of my native City and Country:

An inextinguishable desire to do what I can, in this the eighty-fifth year of my age, impels me to call and fix the attention of the American people on the appalling causes that have so effectually paralyzed the varied industries of our country. This destructive cause has already shrunk the value of property, in less than three years, to a condition where real estate cannot be sold, or mortgages obtained on it, for more than one-half the amount it would have brought, three years ago.

There is nothing that can be more important than to find out and remove a cause that is bringing bankruptcy and ruin on millions of the most industrious and enterprising men of the American people. The national policy that has brought this frightful calamity to our country should receive the most thorough investigation and the most decided action of our Government.

I propose to show the true public policy that underlies this whole question, and to indicate what appears to me as the principles and the just methods that ought to actuate the people, in their exercise of power through the Government, and the remedies which that Government ought to devise. For it must ever be borne in mind that the Government and its policy in this country is just what we, the people, make it. It is our duty, therefore, at all times and in every way, to enlighten and exhort the people, and trust to such appeals, rather than any immediate criticism or direct appeal to the Government itself.

The whole question of the currency and money arises from the necessity of trade or exchanges among men in the products of their industry, and the causes and methods that make these exchanges fair, just, and beneficial to all concerned, or a means of tyranny and injustice, and an occasion for the exercise of greed and selfishness. "A false balance is an abomination to the Lord, but a just weight is His delight." This proverb contains the secret of all unfairness in the dealings between man and man. Justice and truth are at the bottom of all fair exchanges that are beneficial to both parties ; but false balances and unjust weights are the means by which the strong and the insincere oppress or deceive their fellow-men.

Let us then trace, in some simple way, this necessity of exchange among men, and the process by which injustice first creeps in, and the best method of keeping the true balance and the "just weight" in the exchange of one equivalent for the another.

Suppose a community or race of men to have passed that point in their progress when simple barter is any longer the sufficient means of exchange, when some easier and more rapid method must be devised. The first thing selected for this purpose is a concentrated and valuable form of labor, the most portable, durable, and susceptible of carrying on its very face the record and sign of its value. Such is gold and silver money. Its value is two-fold : it is both intrinsic and representative. But it is its representative value that makes it money, or a conventional sign and record of exchanges. So far as its intrinsic value is concerned, the exchange of a piece of gold for anything else is simple barter. But it holds the "balance" even, and it gives a just weight for whatever is exchanged for it, because it has cost labor to produce it.

But there comes a time in the complex and numerous exchanges that take place between men in a higher state of civilization, when even the barter of gold and silver for other products, concentrated and portable as is their intrinsic value, becomes too cumbrous a method, and too slow to effect these exchanges fast enough, and to keep the record of them in the most convenient shape. For this purpose the intrinsic value of the means of exchange is superseded entirely by the representative. The record is taken for a time for the transaction itself, which, however, is assumed will take place infallibly ; and in order to secure a real result of the exchange of values, which at first are the subject of promise and record merely, there must be some real or assumed ability on the part of the one who makes the promise, that he can and will make that promise good. This is the origin of paper money. The value of this paper money, although not intrinsic, as is that of gold and silver, yet is no less real, provided the exchange of values it is used to record can in any way be made certain ; it must hold an "even balance," and be sure to give a "just weight" in the end. But here is the point where deceit and injustice may creep in. The paper money is always representative of value, and a mere sign of a real exchange of values to take place at some future time. It may, hence, be falsified or trusted blindly, and on insufficient grounds. The selfishness and greed of men, or even their groundless hopes and miscalculations, may give a temporary value to this promise to pay, which it cannot sustain. This is the secret of panics, revulsions in business, and prostration of credits. The lie comes to the surface sooner or later, and the credulous find themselves in the snare.

This liability increases in proportion to the want of integrity and commercial intelligence in individuals and communities where such methods of exchange take place. Individuals are less to be trusted with such a vast interest as the power of making paper money, than are corporate bodies of men, and these in turn are less to be trusted than well organized governments. Governments themselves differ very much in this respect, in proportion as they are responsible to the people and easily held in check, or rectified by the demands of public interest. Hence, a true republican government is the safest agency in the world to entrust with the power of making paper money.

A semi-barbarous government, like the Turkish, will, from time to time, even call in all the coin of the country, and reissue it again in a depreciated condition and value. So, paper money is subject to great fluctuations in value, if there be any uncertainty in the real and permanent integrity of the power that issues the paper, or a capricious use of its authority in determining its standard of value.

Experience has shown that individuals cannot be trusted with such a power. Even large corporations cannot be trusted with the common welfare involved in this privilege, and while governments are the safest depositories of the power, they must be such as are not subject either to revolution or to any radical changes of policy, or to any irresponsible exercise of power. This, it appears to me, is now the condition of our Government. Its credit has been, and is now, the support of one of the greatest bonded debts, by means of which the life and the perpetuity of the Union has been secured. The faith of this Government now gives value to an immense paper currency for which the law has provided no redemption. It seems preposterous, therefore, to doubt the ability of this Government to give stability to any currency which it might adopt as indispensable to the welfare of the nation.

That value has hitherto been measured by its exchangeableness with gold, as indicated by the signs of value that are stamped on each, or dollar for dollar. But this is subjecting paper to the laws of barter, as if it had an intrinsic value. It presumes that corporations or governments can control what is uncontrollable, namely, the amount of gold that may, at any time, be in a country.

Gold is diffusible, because it is accepted by all countries as a standard of value and a means of exchange. But it is also fluctuating in any locality by the laws of production, supply, and demand all over the world.

To fix upon an arbitrary and fluctuating standard, such as the worth or exchangeable value of a gold dollar, to indicate the exchangeable power of a paper dollar, is as uncertain as to take any other permanent product of human labor, such as a bushel of wheat or a pound of cotton. Nor can any standard be fixed for the value of a currency, because the uses and demand of currency is a fluctuating want itself. Now, the exchangeable value of anything depends upon its *convertibility into something else* that has value, *at the option of the individual.* This rule applies to paper money as to anything else. But how shall Government give an exchangeable value to a paper currency? Can it do so by a standard which is beyond its control, and which naturally fluctuates, while the sign of exchange indicated by the paper remains the same?

This is the unsound state which possesses the minds of our people and of our politicians.

We must come out of this unreasonable condition, or we shall be subject, for all time, to these periodic disturbances of our money and cur-

rency which bring such widespread ruin and distress on our commer
cial industries, and work on the part of the Government, positive and
cruel injustice. The remedy seems to me to be very plain.

First.—We must put this whole power of coining money or issuing
currency, as Thomas Jefferson says, "where, by the Constitution, it
properly belongs"—entirely in the hands of our Government. That
Government is a republic; hence it is under control of the people.
Corporations and States have hitherto, in some form or other, divided
this power with the Government. Hence come the embarrassments and
the fluctuations, as may be easily shown.

But now we must trust our Government with this *whole function* of
providing the standards and measures of exchange, as we trust it with
the weights and measures of all trade. So far from putting the people
in the power of our Government and at the caprice of parties in power,
I contend, it will bring the Government more under the control of the
people and give a check to mere party rule. For the more stake the
people have in the wisdom and honesty of the administration of the
Government, the more watchful and firm they will be in its control.

Secondly.—We must require the Government to make this currency,
at all times, and at the option of the individual, *redeemable.* The
Government can redeem its promises to pay in three ways—by its
taxes, its bonds, and by coin. The taxes are just as sound and true a
method of redemption, as the real *debts against a man are an equivalent
for his notes.* For when a man pays his taxes, with paper, he pays
what he owes the Government in evidences of debt, on the part of the
Government.

Furthermore, the Government may redeem its notes, in bonds.
This method, although it is paying one debt by another, is redemption by a form more desirable to the holder; because, one is an interest bearing debt, and the other is not. But to prevent the
currency from running all into bonds, two regulations are necessary,
first that the bonds should be *reconvertible* into currency; and secondly,
that the bonds should bear a lower rate of interest, than the average of
safe investments in active business. The Government has entire control over its bonds, to which it can give a definite as well as a permanent value. These are, in fact, a mortgage upon the embodied wealth
of the whole country. The reality of their value is as sound and as
permanent as the Government itself, and the degree of their value can
be determined exactly by the amount of interest the Government may
think proper to fix.

This convertibility will always keep a check, both in the amount of
currency and the amount of bonds that may be called for at any time;
for the bonds are property, creating an income, and the currency is
merely the measure of property and the means of exchange. If currency
swells in the hands of the people, it will show that business is active,
exchanges numerous, and investments profitable. If currency shrinks
and bonds increase, it will only be to the extent of those natural fluctuations which seasons and times bring upon the productive energies
of man. But at no time will either the bonds or the currency be a
mere drug upon the market, for they will be mutually *convertible.*

Lastly, the Government can afford to redeem its paper in coin, if it be also the *exclusive* paper money of the country; if it be the *only* legal tender for debts, and if it be received by the Government for all taxes and dues, and convertible, at par, with the bonds of the Government, at the will of the holder; for then, the currency would be *on a par with gold and silver.* But the Government can never afford to do this unless *all these conditions are observed,* with regard to its currency. The Government can have no other control than these conditions give over the relations between paper and coin, except that of changing the *standard weight of the coin dollar.* This has been done by Governments, with advantage to the interests of trade, many times, in the history of coining, because the demands of trade and commerce have outgrown the supply of the precious metals, and it became necessary to redivide the coin as a standard of value. The precious metals are now used mostly to pay "balances" in the commerce of nations; and this *very use disqualifies them from being the domestic currency of any nation.* But a certain quantity of gold and silver, subject to recoining from time to time, will be always very convenient as a standard and measure *for a unit of value* in the currency.

When we look into the history of the past for the real cause of those periodical panics, that have brought financial ruin on so many of our people, we find that on all those occasions, as in the present paralyzed condition of the trade and commerce of the country, the main difficulty has originated in the unfortunate financial policy adopted by the General Government—a policy that is producing for our people what the policy of the British Government has brought about for the people of that country, where the real estate of the whole of England has, in a comparatively short period, been transferred from 165,000 of the past, to 30,000 land-owners of the present. And this, where the most rapid increase of wealth, perhaps, in the world, is also attended with the worst and most unequal distribution; and where, instead of a diffused happiness and universal prosperity, the rich grow richer and the poor poorer, by constant vacillations in the measures of value.

Our own Government, instead of taking the whole subject of money and currency entirely in its hands, as provided for by the Constitution, allowed, for a time, local banks to multiply and continue until their notes, which were promises to pay specie on demand, became mere delusions, and the best informed and most prudent merchant found it impossible to distinguish those that were redeemable, or convertible into gold, from those that were not. The chartered Bank of the United States, in the first four years of its operation, issued $40,000,000 of paper with only $300,000 in specie to redeem its notes. Banks evaded the law by issuing paper that they were unable to redeem. The reason of this lay in the fact that the demand for currency at times was far in excess of the quantity that could be reabsorbed into gold, when the currency was no longer needed.

Gold alone, was not its proper agent of conversion, because it is uncertain in volume, and is itself subject to the magnetic attraction of a foreign trade that needs it to make up its balances.

Had the currency, which should have been all United States currency, been at once convertible into United States bonds, which, instead of locking it up, as would be the case now, should have given a small interest, until the currency was wanted again, when the bonds should *immediately* be convertible into currency, we would have escaped the panics and stagnation of trade and stoppage of industry which has now affected the commerce of the world.

The local banks were allowed to continue until the war of the rebellion compelled the Government to issue a currency as legal tender, as the only advisable means of carrying on its operations for the safety of the nation's life.

In this extremity our Government was literally compelled, as a war measure, to offer to these local banks nearly double the ordinary interest of loans, in order to induce them to lend their money to the Government, and base their banking on the bonds of the Government, and exchange their own currency for that of the United States. This great advantage given to capital invested in the local banks should have come to an end when the war was over, as it was only a war measure. At the end of the war, common justice to the debtor class should have prevented the Government from doing anything to lessen the purchasing power of those legal-tender notes which the people had been literally compelled to accept for all products of their labor. The circulation should have been left simply to the natural law. At the close of the war, the legal tenders should have been made the permanent currency of the country, and the volume should not have been increased or diminished, except as *per capita*, with the increase of the population of the country. And further, it should have been made convertible into the bonds of the Government, over which it has entire control, and to which it could give a permanent value in interest. Instead of this, what do we find the Government doing? Resolving that at a certain future time, in 1879, the currency shall be convertible into gold! Why did not our Congressmen proceed to resolve that, by that time, there should be gold enough in the country to absorb all the currency that foreigners and importers might wish to be converted into gold? But this they could not do. Hence the present unwillingness of capital to invest in business or manufacture, because the capitalist does not know what his property or his money may be worth, four years hence. This currency must be made convertible, or it cannot measure real property, or properly represent it. But its convertibility into gold cannot be made a matter of legal enactment, until the other conditions are observed, as above stated, which will make our currency on a par with gold. For this purpose, I would demonetize gold and silver, altogether except as tokens of value, and have nothing but its paper, the legal tender of the country. The paper then would be of such *indispensable* use that what was needed to be turned into specie, could be converted at par.

The only policy the Government could adopt to influence the influx of gold into this country, and keep its relations on a par with other commodities and with the paper currency, would be that the Government should require its import duties to be paid in legal tenders, **adding always the premium on gold** to the amount as estimated in the paper currency. That would be desirable at present, or until the national debt is extinguished, because the Government is under obligation to pay the interest of its bonds in gold. It will have a tendency to keep the paper on a par with gold; for it will make it easier to pay the dues of the Government; besides, the superior convenience and *certain convertibility* of the paper will always have a tendency to keep it on a par, or even make it more valuable than gold. But interest-bearing bonds are purely a subject of legal enactment, and hence can be controlled by the Government. This is the whole secret of the difficulty, and the real key to our financial condition. Our currency, in point of fact, is not convertible into gold. When it is not needed, as at present, to the full extent of its volume to effect the exchanges or pay the wages of labor, because these are in a measure interrupted, what is to be done with it? Some say, "Call it in and burn it up," that the rest may be worth its own volume in gold. But this currency has already been in circulation; it is now the measure of the whole property of the country, and has been the measure of many exchanges, and now represents the great mass of indebtedness. To bring down its relative value to that of gold is as arbitrary a measure, as to bring it to the standard of any other product—that of wheat or iron, for instance.

It will place all in the power of those who have the most gold. It will transfer a large part of the property of the country to foreigners, or to those who can readily draw gold from Europe.

But let us consider this subject more closely. If we admit that there is at any one time only a certain amount of gold in the world, it is certain that our community or nation cannot obtain more than its share without leaving all the others in a deficiency—at least for a time.

By this means one nation has the power to derange the exchanges, and through these, the industries of every other country. The caprice and power even of a few large capitalists can do this. It would be, therefore, an unwise policy for our government to allow this one article of gold, that all nations are struggling to obtain by the use of all the arts that human ingenuity can devise, and which must be employed in settling all balances of trade between different countries, and which, as a product of nature and of human industry, is uncontrollable by any law that the government can devise—to make this the standard of all values and the legalized measure of all trade and exchange in this country, would be in direct opposition to the opinion of many of the wisest statesmen that our country has produced. This will appear by the following expression of their views:

JEFFERSON.

Vol. VI., p. 199, Jefferson's works, letter to Mr. Eppis.

"*Bank paper must be suppressed, and the circulating medium* must be *restored to the nation to whom it belongs.* It is the only fund on which they can rely for loans; it is the only resource which can never fail them, and it is an abundant one for every necessary purpose. *Treasury bills, bottomed on taxes, bearing or not bearing interest, as may be found necessary, thrown into circulation, will take the place of so much gold or silver*, which last, when crowded, will find an efflux into other countries, and thus keep the quantum of medium at its salutary level."

Also the great statesman and philosopher, Benjamin Franklin, in Vol. IV., page 82, of his work, says: "Gold and silver are not intrinsically of equal value with iron. Their value rests chiefly in the estimation they happen to be in, among the generality of nations. Any other well-founded credit is as much an equivalent as gold and silver. Paper money, well founded, has great advantages over gold and silver, being light and convenient for handling large sums, and not likely to have its volume reduced by demands for exportation. On the whole, no method has hitherto been formed to establish a medium of trade equal in all its advantages to bills of credit made a general legal-tender."

JOHN C. CALHOUN'S OPINION.

The following is an extract from a speech of Hon. John C. Calhoun, in the Senate of the United States, on the currency issue, and is eminently appropriate to be quoted in the prevailing discussion. Mr. Calhoun said, Vol. III., p. 83:

"It appears to me, after bestowing the best reflection I can give the subject, that no convertible paper—that is, no paper whose credit rests on the promise to pay coin—is suitable for a currency. It is the form of credit proper in private transactions between man and man, but not for a standard of value, to perform exchanges generally, which constitutes the approximate function of money, or currency." Then on page 87: "No one can doubt but that the Government credit is better than that of any bank—more stable and more safe. . . . Bank paper is cheap to those who make it, but dear, very dear, to those who use it. On the other hand the credit of the Government, while it would greatly facilitate its financial operations, would cost nothing, or next to nothing, both to it and the people, and would, of course, add nothing to the cost of production, which would give every branch of our industries—agriculture, commerce, and manufactures, as far as its circulation might extend, great advantages both at home and abroad; . . . and I now undertake to affirm, and without the least fear that I can be answered, that a paper issued by government, with the simple promise to receive it for all its dues, leaving its creditors to take it, or gold or silver, at their option, would, to the extent it could circulate, form a perfect paper circulation, which could not be abused by the Government; that it would be as uniform in value as the metals themselves; and I shall be able to prove that it is within the Constitution and powers of Congress to use such a paper in the management of its finances, according to the most rigid rule of construing the Constitution."

SPENCER ON FINANCE.

Herbert Spencer stands among the first writers and thinkers of this age. He studies and writes for the sake of the truth. Hence the following from his pen will be fresh and invigorating to thirsty souls of this time. Vol. VIII., p. a33:

" The monetary arrangements of any community are ultimately de
pendent, like most other arrangements, on the morality of its members.
Amongst a people altogether dishonest, every mercantile transaction
must be effected in coin or goods ; for promises to pay cannot circulate
at all when, by the hypothesis, there is no probability that they will
be redeemed. Conversely, amongst perfectly honest people, paper alone
will form the circulating medium, and metallic money will be needless.
Manifestly, therefore, during any intermediate state, in which men are
neither altogether dishonest nor altogether honest, a mixed currency will
exist ; and the ratio of paper to coin will vary with the degree of trust
individuals place in each other.

" There seems no evading this conclusion. The greater the preva-
lence of fraud, the greater will be the number of transactions in which
the seller will part with his goods only for an equivalent of intrinsic
value ; that is, the greater will be the number of transactions in which
coin is required, and the more will the metallic currency preponderate.
On the other hand, the more generally men find each other trustworthy,
the more frequently will they take payment in notes, bills of exchange,
and checks ; the fewer will be the cases in which gold and silver are
called for, and the smaller will be the quantity of gold and silver in
circulation."

RICARDO.

" The pretensions of those who are attempting to drive this country
back to the barbarism of a metallic basis for our currency are fast giving away for want of argument. It is being discovered that all the
great writers who have analyzed the subject, and viewed it from a scientific stand-point, came to the conclusion that paper is superior to metal
for a currency. Even Ricardo, the high priest of the bullionists, the
father of the present British system, allows this. He says :

" A regulated paper currency is so great an improvement in commerce that I should greatly regret if prejudice should induce us to return to a system of less utility. The introduction of the precious
metals for the purposes of money may with truth be considered as one
of the most important steps towards the improvement of commerce and
the arts of civilized life. But it is no less true that, with the advancement of knowledge and science, we discover that it would be another
improvement to banish them again from the employment to which,
during the less enlightened period, they had been so advantageously
applied."

HORACE GREELEY'S PLAN.

" Let Congress make our greenbacks fundable at the pleasure of the
holder, in bonds of $100, $1,000, and $10,000, drawing interest at the
rate of one cent a day on each $100 (or $3.65 per annum), and exchangeable into greenbacks at the pleasure of the holder. Now authorize the
Treasurer to purchase and extinguish our outstanding bonds, so fast as
it is supplied with the means of so doing by receipts for customs or
otherwise, and to issue new greenbacks whenever large amounts shall be

required, every one being fundable in sums of $100, $1,000, or $10,000, as aforesaid, at the pleasure of the holder, in bonds drawing an annual interest of $3.65 in coin per annum, and these bonds exchangeable into greenbacks whenever a holder shall desire it.

"Our greenbacks, which are now virtual falsehoods, would be truths. The Government would pay them on demand in bonds as aforesaid, which is in substantial accordance with the plan on which the greenbacks were first authorized."

It appears by a speech of W. W. Allen, Esq., that there had been drawn from the people, in the shape of taxes and duties, during eight years between the 31st of August, 1865, and the 1st of November, 1873, the amount of $631,488,677, making a reduction of the national debt in eight years of $631,488,677, showing that an annual amount of $195,113,356 has been drawn from the people in the shape of taxes and paid towards the extinguishment of our national debt. This amount was over and above the amount drawn from the people to pay all the expenses of the Government, in addition to the amount required to pay the interest on the national debt.

Such a rapid withdrawal of the people's means from their ordinary business is quite sufficient to account for the ruin now brought on untold thousands of the American people.

For our Government to continue such a policy and go on drawing taxes from the people as they have done, to extinguish the national debt before it is either due or wanted by those who hold it, is about as wise as it was for Pharaoh to expect his people to make bricks without straw.

The people could and would willingly have paid the five dollars interest on every hundred dollars of the national debt. They could have paid the interest on the debt with enough of the principal to show that they honestly intended to pay the whole amount.

This they could and would have done if they had been permitted to retain the tools of their trades; the amount of currency on which they were compelled to depend for their ability to pay the taxes on the cost of the war.

I believe I have shown that the policy adopted by our Government to hasten a return to specie payments has rendered the attainment of that object more distant and difficult than it was at the close of the war of the rebellion.

I am now convinced that an opposite policy, one that would have legalized all the Government money in circulation at the close of the war, making it convertible into interest-bearing bonds, and reconvertible into currency at the will of the holder, would have established justice between the people and the Government, and would have caused our currency to appreciate to the value of gold long before this. It would have left the money, the sinews of war, the tools of trade, in the hands of the people, to enable them to meet the expenses incurred, and make the necessary provisions for the hundreds of thousands of disbanded soldiers thrown back on their homes to find employment or starve.

In conclusion, I would say that we have every reason to hope for our country. But we must not trust in the amount of our gold or other riches, but in the principles of our Constitution as free people, and in the free development of all our magnificent resources. We must turn again the tide of immigration which is now leaving our shores. We can do this, as in the past, by continuing to offer a better reward for labor, and cheaper land for settlement, by a faithful administration of our laws in the interests of the people, and not of classes or monopolies, and by trusting in all questions of money and currency to the integrity and power of our Government, and not placing ourselves at the mercy of foreign capitalists nor submitting tamely to that war of commerce which every nation is willing to make upon us, if we do not take effectual means for our own self-preservation.

A LETTER ADDRESSED IN 1875.

To the Editor of the "Evening Post:"

In some of your late issues, I find an article by S. S. P., entitled "Peter Cooper's New Departure," and an article with a similar title, by my old and valued friend, John B. Jarvis. These communications allude to the fact that, seventeen years ago, I held it to be unsafe for the public welfare, as I now do, to allow banks to incur liabilities, payable in specie, on demand, by issues of paper and loans many times the amount of the specie they held in their vaults, or could obtain from any source, for the immediate payment of their notes in gold, on demand. This demand was made with all the accompanying disasters of widespread ruin and interruption of credit and industry, in times called "panics." The effect of the panic of 1857, and the causes, are very clearly detailed in Mr. Caldwell's work on "Ways and Means of Payment"—p. 485.

Gold is a commodity, and a product of industry. Its value is determined, like that of any other commodity, by supply and demand. Why not let those who need it pay the price? Why should the necessary facilities of the *home trade* be contracted, whenever there is a demand for gold for export? This it is that subjects the whole country, from time to time, to a fall or derangement in prices and an interruption to business? Even with our present irredeemable legal-tenders, all must see that when gold varies five per cent. in a few days, neither the value of these legal-tenders, as measured by other property, nor the rest of the property of the country is perceptibly affected. My " New Departure," as my friends term it, is the result of observation and experience. I should be sorry to be among those who learn nothing from the past. "Hard money," or what is equivalent to it, a paper currency at all times redeemable in gold and silver, can no longer be relied on to answer the wants of this country. But I am as much opposed to an irredeemable currency, and an inflated and irresponsible paper money as I ever was. Our experience, as a nation, should have taught us by this time, by the "panics" of the past and the oft-repeated failures of banks, that these banks are utterly unable to redeem their notes in specie whenever gold is wanted of them in any large quantities. It is evident that there is some intrinsic difficulty about this redemption in specie, beyond the power either of banks or of Government to control. except by methods not yet adopted by Government. I trust that my friend John B. Jarvis and S. S. P. will find, on a more careful examination of what I have written, that I am as much opposed to an irresponsible, inflated, paper currency, as I ever was. I am now opposed to the present currency, so far as it is irredeemable; but I am also opposed to the policy of withdrawing the currency from circulation, until the residue shall be on a par with gold, because that would work great injustice to the debtor class. I do not believe in the good policy of selling Government bonds, as a means of resuming specie payments, as it will soon be drained from us again, leaving our paper as it was before, irredeemable in gold; nor in the purchase of silver to take the place of the best small currency our country has ever possessed. It is a currency that is now serving the country without interest; and is giving back to the whole people whatever is *lost or worn out* in the public service. But let the currency at all times be exchangeable with *interest-bearing bonds*, and let the Government not only make its money a legal tender, but receive it for all dues, and we shall hear no more either of "inflation" or of "depreciation." This is my doctrine "in a nutshell." I believe with Jefferson and many of our wisest statesmen, that our general Government is as much bound by the Constitution to hold the entire control of all that is allowed as a legal money measure, in the regulation of trade and commerce, as they are bound to fix a standard for the pound weight or the bushel measure. That this measure of value should be made as unfailing and unalterable as possible. And the currency should always compare well with the most condensed and valuable form of human labor, as it is now found in gold. But after the most mature reflection, I find myself compelled to believe, with Benjamin Franklin, "that any other well-founded credit is as much an equivalent for labor as gold and silver." He says, what all now know to be true, "that paper money, *well founded*, has great advantage over gold and silver, being light and convenient for handling in large sums, and not likely to have its volume reduced by demands for exportation." "On the whole," he says, "no method has hitherto been found to establish a medium of trade equal, in all its advantages, *to bills of credit made a general legal tender."*

That such a policy is practicable is proved by the fact that the French Government has made and maintained a legal tender paper circulation, through one of the fiercest and, to them, the most disastrous wars of modern times; and, having paid a thousand millions of indemnity, their paper money is to-day nearly on a par with gold. This is because the Government took its own paper for all dues, instead of discrediting it, by not taking it, as ours does. They take their paper also for French Government bonds, which has resulted in the public debt being mainly due to their own citizens, instead of foreigners, as ours is to-day, thus becoming a perpetual tax on the resources of the country.

My efforts to avoid the evils that have befallen the finances of our country, will appear in a paragraph from a petition sent by me to Con gress.

"During the session of the Congress of 1869, I had the honor to send to every member of the Senate and House of Representatives a plan for the establishment of a currency that all our experience has shown to be the best that our country has ever possessed. It only required an act of Congress declaring that the legal tenders then in circulation should never be increased or diminished in amount, only as *per capita*, with the increase of inhabitants of the country. It will now only require an act of Congress to make such currency as just and permanent a measure of the value of all property and labor, as the yard-stick or pound weight, as money, weight, and measure must always exist by governmental authority. To make our present legal tenders the best currency in the world, it will only require that Congress receive the legal tenders in payment for all duties with an amount of currency added that will be equal to the premium that gold has borne during the month preceding the maturing of all contracts. This plan will make it the interest of every man to bring legal tenders on a par with gold in the shortest possible time."

The several quotations of the opinions of eminent men in the history of this country, which I gave in my "Letter on the Currency," were intended to show by good authority that Congress had a right to borrow money on the credit of the United States, and to issue bonds bearing interest for the same; and in this is implied the power to issue a currency as legal tender, for this is only another form of the public debt. But to incur the great debt of four hundred millions of dollars in the shape of a paper currency; to make this a "forced loan," by making this paper a legal tender for all debts as between individuals, and to pay it to every one from whom the Government obtained service or material, and at the same time to discredit this paper, by refusing to take it for the Government dues, and to withdraw forty-four millions of this currency from the active trade of the people in the course of two or three years, thus embarrassing trade and shrinking values, until a "*panic*" was brought on: all this seems to me a great mistake on the part of our Government—not the issuing of this currency, for that was a necessary war measure to save the integrity of the Union—but to make this currency irredeemable, either in bonds or in gold; and then to contract it, after all values had been measured by this currency for some years, and debts incurred which the parties had the right to believe were to be paid in good faith, by the same measure as they were contracted—this does seem to me not only a great mistake, but a great injustice to the people.

I have urgently recommended that our Government should hold itself bound, as an inviolable obligation, to regard every dollar of the legal tenders, which were issued to save the nation's life as a loan drawn from the people, which the Government was as much bound to pay in full measure as ever a debt due from one individual to another. This debt was a fair claim on the whole property of the country. When made a legal tender, it should have been received by the Government for all dues, and the whole amount issued should have been allowed to become the permanent standard and measure of all values, as it was for a time, letting the natural demands of trade and commerce and the gradual growth of the country determine its future value, as compared with other commodities—gold, for instance.

This currency should have for its base of security the solemn pledge, already given by the Government, that the $400,000,000 and other national currency put in circulation as a war debt should never be increased, unless called for by conditions just as imperative as war. And further, this pledge should have been followed by an act of Congress, to tax the whole property of the country, on which this war debt was a lien, to pay the interest of it at some proper rate to those who held the currency, but could not use it advantageously in trade, by making it convertible into bonds at any time at the will of the holder. Such a course would have give an annual assurance that our Government meant to pay every dollar of its debt, both at home and abroad. It would also have given to our country a degree of stability in the operations of trade and commerce, that would in time compensate our country for all the losses occasioned by the war of rebellion.

In conclusion, I would say that ever since paper money was issued by any civilized country, except, perhaps, at the very first, it has soon grown out of all possible redemption in coin alone. So that it has generally been assumed that one dollar in coin would float from three to five dollars in paper. But this has only been true in the times of expanding credits. As soon as contraction came, for any cause, a "panic ensued;" for it was found that a dollar in coin was needed for every dollar in paper. Why, then, keep up this vain fiction any longer? It can only serve to expand credits to an unwarrantable degree, while it permits another class to contract credits suddenly and to a ruinous degree. It leads inevitably to "panics." Now, it seems to me there is a plain way out of all these financial difficulties. If currency is issued only as an equivalent of bonds, then every dollar of the currency is at all times sustained, or "floated," by an equal value of the bonds of the Government. An "expansion of currency" can go no further than the actual equivalent received by the Government for its bonds. A "contraction of currency" can go on no faster than the conversion of the paper into bonds. Panics will be impossible, because there will always be a means by which real "assets" can be at once converted into money. It is this want of "ready conversion" that causes panics and ruins even "well-founded houses." I have said before, that I believe this will bring the currency on a par with gold; but whether it does or not, it is certain that we cannot, by any legal enactments, keep our currency on a par with gold, without either shrinking its volume to less than the ordinary demands of trade and commerce in this country and doing great injustice to the debtor class, or by a proper policy on the part of the Government in respect to this currency, to prevent those great fluctuations in its value which lie at the foundation of all financial troubles.

I have lived too long to enter now, at this late day of my protracted life, into the mere partisan disputes of the day. I have no other object or interest than the welfare of the whole people of my country; and, believing as I do, I should hold myself very much to blame, if I with held my feeble testimony in this important crisis of the country, and on a question involving such momentous consequences as a sound currency and a true financial system. On these we must depend for the future prosperity and happiness of the whole industrial class, with whom I have ever been in sympathy. I confess to a most profound anxiety for all those who, with their best efforts, find life a great struggle for a bare subsistence.

These troubles will be greatly lessened when gold becomes, as it should be, only a guide in the exchanges of commerce, as the mariner looks at the north star as his best guide over a dangerous ocean.

THE CURRENCY QUESTION.

The following address was prepared by Peter Cooper for delivery at the meeting of the Union League Club at New York City. It contains a full exposition of his views on financial questions. We recommend its careful reading and consideration:

Mr. President and Gentlemen of the Union League Club:

I find myself impelled by an irresistible desire to call and fix the attention of every lover of his kind and country on those appalling causes that have so effectually paralyzed the varied industries of our people. Those causes have been sufficient to shrink the real estate of the nation to one-half the amount it would have brought three years ago; and that without having shrunk at the same time any of the debts that had been contracted by the use of money authorized by the Government of our country. There is nothing that can be more important than to find out and remove the causes that are bringing bankruptcy and ruin to the homes of millions of the most industrious men of our nation. The national policy that has brought this frightful calamity on our people should receive the most thorough investigation and the most decided action by the Government of our country. There is but one way of relief out of all this national trouble and sorrow. The people themselves must enforce upon the administration the obligations laid down in the Constitution, "to establish justice, and thus secure the general welfare of the nation." To do this, let us take it out of the power of States or corporations to make or unmake the money of the country. It is the sole duty of the Government to coin money, as the Constitution requires. Let the Government itself, through its Administration, be restrained from meddling capriciously with the currency, and only under permanent laws and a well-understood and predetermined policy, always having reference to the good of the people.

Let us have a national currency, issued solely by the authority and supported in circulation by the taxing power and the solvency of our Government. Such a currency should be fixed in volume, as *per capita*, to the amount of the people's money actually found in circulation at the close of the war, and it should be made as certain and as permanent in value in its measuring power as the yard, pound, and bushel, by its being made redeemable for all Government taxes, duties, and debts, as well as a legal tender for all private debts. This currency must be always interconvertible with Government bonds at a low rate of interest, as compared with active investment. It should be a currency which a bank or corporation cannot rightfully issue, enlarge, or contract in its own interest, and which cannot be taken from the hands of the people by the "ever-shifting balance of commodities" between nations, as is the case with gold and silver when used as money. It will not be subject to any sudden contractions or expansions, but will be regulated by established law, based on scientific facts and principles of a just system of national finances. The greenback can be made just such a currency. This currency can always be kept on an average par with gold or the currency of any other country by the encouragement and the support which it will give to the industry and the productiveness of the country. It will increase indefinitely the country's exporting power. We will then pay our "balances" with other nations with our surplus products, and have but little occasion for the use of gold and silver to pay balances of trade. We can in no way become an exporting nation except by stimulating our own productiveness, diversified and enlarged in every direction of human industry, in which our materials are as good and abundant as those of other nations, and the labor and skill are ready for use if properly encouraged. For this purpose I believe it will be wise for us to remove all internal taxation, and rely solely on a sufficient revenue tariff to meet the expenses of Government. This subject is very much misunderstood or misrepresented by our own advocates of free trade. It is the surplus productions of foreign countries mostly that reach our shores as imports, and it is also the surplus capital of the importers and the foreigners that is employed to bring them here. Hence it is but right to tax this "surplus" for the absolute wants of our own domestic industry and capital. This is precisely what a tariff accomplishes. It taxes the importer and the foreigner chiefly, who must find a market somewhere; and those of our people who will buy and use foreign products, who leave our own good raw materials unused, and our own domestic laborers unemployed. This is violating the first law of nature—self-preservation. Let us take care of our own people here at home as the first duty of our own Government. And let us not make the great mistake of the governing classes in France, England, and Germany, where the wages of the operatives and workingmen are reduced to a bare subsistence.

It is this ignorance or want of patriotism that stands in the way of the public weal, both in the management of our finances and the adoption of a judicious tariff. The people alone can vindicate their rights and secure their own welfare by taking an intelligent and proper interest in the administration of their own Government. Let them require from this Administration a return to the principles of public justice and equal rights. Let the Government be required in some proper way to restore to the people the tools of their trade and commerce, which have been so unjustly and cruelly taken from them. Let there be provision made for the return of the whole of that currency found in circulation at the close of the rebellion, which was worked out and paid for by the people in the labor, material, and service which they had rendered to the Government during our struggle for the nation's life. It was a currency which had lifted the American people into a state of unexampled prosperity, never before known in this or any other country, and which can be restored to the people by the issue of greenbacks paid out for the necessary expenses of Government, for the execution of great necessary international works, such as the Northern and Southern Pacific railroads, which, when made, will strengthen the bonds of the Union, and open a vast country, with its untold wealth, for the enterprise and labor of the people. I have sounded these notes of encouragement, warning, and advice time and again, because I believe they are for the peace and happiness of our country. At my advanced age I have no personal ambition or motive left but the welfare of mankind and the prosperity of my beloved country. If it were the last word I should utter with my dying breath, I should warn the people of this country against the insidious wiles of professed politicians, who are seeking for the spoils of office and the attractions of power—men who are ready to lend themselves to all special and partial acts of legislation, if they can only advance their own individual interests. Such men oppose " civil service " because it will curtail their political patronage ; such men barter the rights, the prosperity, and even the bread of the people, in order to share in the spoils and the temporary gains which are thrown into the hands of a few by a pernicious system of banking, of which the periodical panics of our country bear a frightful record. They are the natural outgrowth of the same injurious system.

My arguments will be confirmed by a reference to the facts stated in the following letter in relation to the currency by F. E. Spinner, the former United States Treasurer. Mr. Spinner says that there was put in circulation, in all the forms of six per cent., five per cent., and 3.65 per cent., of legal tender money, $1,152,924,892, besides the seven-thirties, $830,000,000, which Mr. Spinner says were intended, prepared, and used as currency. This amount had been paid out as so many dollars, and had become the people's money, which the Government was then and forever bound to receive from the people as legal tender dollars for every form of taxes, duties, and debts. The failure of the Government to do that duty has cost the nation thousands of millions of dollars. It will be recollected by many members of this club that we were favored on a former occasion by Prof. White, of Cornell University, with an account of the losses sustained by the people of France by the use of the assignats authorized by that Government. I have always regretted that my esteemed friend, Prof. White, had not gone far enough into the true history of the rise, progress, and use of the assignats of France, to see that the injurious losses occasioned by them did not arise from an improper action of the republican Government, but by the combined powers of the internal and external enemies of the Republic. This will appear by the following facts : The assignats of France were based on the confiscated property of the clergy and nobility, in which both the clergy and the nobility had a deep interest, that led them to denounce the assignat as based on theft and outrage. There was another royal party that united in declaring that their lands had been taken without any of the forms of law, and therefore the title still remained in the clergy. The parties all united in declaring that the assignats were utterly without basis to secure their redemption. The parties never ceased to agitate war on the credit of the assignats. But finding the Revolution too strong for them, and that its cause was being so successfully strengthened by conquering the enemies of liberty and of the nation, that other nations were yielding to its power, and that its armies were victorious, and that its principles, as developed by the constitution and laws, were such as reason and humanity approved, history tells us that all. the enemies of the new French Government united in an effort to destroy the power of the new Government by circulating counterfeit assignats in every direction. The counterfeiting commenced in 1792 in Belgium and Switzerland, and was used extensively as the best means of destroying the power of the Republic. It was found by the nobility that Belgium and Switzerland were too much in sympathy with the revolutionists to be trusted. They then extended their operations to London, where they found more scope and greater opportunities for uninterrupted work. History charges that England lent her aid by allowing "seventeen manufacturing establishments in operation in London, with a force of 400 men, in the production of the assignats."

It was found that 12,000,000,000 of counterfeit francs had been circulated in France, when only 7,860,000,000 of francs had been issued by the Government, showing that the danger of an over-issue was from the enemies of the Government, and not from the Government itself. The assessed value of the property on which was based the 7,860,000,000 of francs was, in 1795, 15,000,000,000, showing that as long as the confiscation of property was maintained by the Government the assignats had good security for their redemption.

It is more than probable that we shall see again what are called "prosperous times," when the banks have annihilated our greenback currency, and have substituted their own money, on the old and false pretence of a "specie basis," which makes their money "as good as gold" until the gold is really wanted. But I warn my countrymen that this will be a baseless prosperity, that can only last while there are any securities or property that can be pledged for loans, the loans themselves being puffed up under the conceit that they are payable in gold; then another crash will come, and we shall have the same scenes of desolation and suffering that we have experienced as a people for the past three years. I do most earnestly beseech the American people to to see to it that their chosen rulers are men imbued with the spirit and letter of the Constitution, which, after a great struggle, was enacted "to establish justice, promote the general welfare, and secure the blessings of liberty to ourselves and our posterity."

PETER COOPER.

AN OPEN LETTER

TO

THE PRESIDENT OF THE UNITED STATES

BY

PETER COOPER.

New York, June 1st, 1877.

HONORED SIR:

Allow me to offer you my heartfelt thanks for the wise and independent course you have adopted in the discharge of the responsible and difficult duties that you have been called upon to perform. The deep interest you are manifesting in the nation's welfare has already sent a thrill of hope and joy into the heart of suffering millions throughout our country. They are looking to you with anxious hope that you will urgently recommend and insist upon the "establishment of justice" in the dealings of the Government with the people; as that is the only possible way by which the general "welfare of the nation can be promoted."

Your noble course has, thus far, inspired the people with the hope and trust that you will, in the providence of God, be our country's Moses, to lead the people from a threatened bondage that now hangs over the liberties and the happiness of the American people.

This bondage has its manifold centre and its secret force in more than two thousand banks that are scattered throughout the country. All these banks are organized expressly to loan out their own money and the money of all those who will entrust them with deposits. These loans are made to men whose business-lives will soon become dependent on money borrowed from corporations that have a special interest of their own. Such a power of wealth, under the control of the selfish instincts of mankind, will always be able to control the action of our Government, unless that Government is directed by strict principles of justice and of the public welfare. The banks will favor a course of special and partial legislation in order to increase their power—"for even the good want power"; they will never cease to ask for more, as long as there is more that can be wrung from the toiling masses of the American people.

Such a power should never be allowed to go out from the entire and complete control of the people's government. The struggle with this money-power, intrenched in the special privileges of banks, has been going on from the beginning of the history of this country. It has engaged the attention of our wisest and most patriotic statesmen. Franklin, Jefferson, Webster, Calhoun, Jackson, have all spoken of the danger of such a power and the necessity of guarding against it.

In the opinion of Thomas Jefferson, the Constitution has made this subject clear, plain, and positive. He says: " Bank paper *must be suppressed*, and the *circulation must be restored* to the nation, to whom it belongs."

The great delusion and the snare of the banks is " a specie convertible paper," which they can never convert when the specie is most wanted. On this point Benjamin Franklin declares that a national " paper money, well-founded, has great advantages over gold and silver, being light and easy to handle in large sums, and not likely to have its volume reduced by demands for exportation." " On the whole," he says, "no method has hitherto been discovered to establish a medium of trade equal in all its advantages to bills of credit made a general legal tender."

John C. Calhoun declares that, "after bestowing the best reflection I can give the subject, that no convertible paper is suitable for a currency. It is the form of credit proper in private transactions between man and man, but not for a standard of value, to perform exchanges generally, which constitutes the appropriate function of currency, or money." Then, on page 87, he says : " *No one* can doubt but that the Government credit *is better than that of any bank – more stable and more safe.* . . . Bank-paper is cheap to those who make it, but dear, very dear, to those who use it. On the other hand, the credit of the Government, while it would greatly facilitate its financial operations, would cost nothing, or next to nothing, both to it and the people, and would, of course, add nothing to the cost of production, which would give every branch of our industries—agriculture, commerce, and manufactures—as far as its circulation might extend, great advantages both at home and abroad ; . . . and I now undertake to affirm, and without the least fear that I can be answered, that a paper issued by Government, with the simple promise to receive it for all its dues, leaving its creditors to take it, or gold and silver, at their option, would, to the extent it could circulate, form a perfect paper circulation which could not be abused by the Government ; that it would be as uniform in value as the metals themselves. And I shall be able to prove that it is within the Constitution and powers of Congress to use such a paper in the management of its finances, according to the most rigid rule of construing the Constitution."

The present Secretary of the Treasury, speaking in the Senate, when the subject of regulating the currency was under consideration, declared it to be a fact, that "every citizen of the United States had conformed his business to the legal-tender clause." That Senator further declared, as appears by the "Congressional Record," that "if the bondholder refuses to take the same kind of money with which he bought the bonds, he is an extortioner and a repudiator. . . . There is no such burdensome loan negotiated by any civilized nation in the world as our five-twenty bonds if they are to be paid in gold." And yet these very six per cent. bonds, that were issued under a law that made them payable in the currency of the country, have by a *most cruel and unaccountable* change in the law, been made payable in gold—the very bonds which had been sold at from forty to sixty dollars in gold for one hundred in currency, thereby causing a debt that now hangs like a millstone on the neck of the nation. It should always be remembered that debt, in all the ages of the world, has been the most effectual means for holding the mass of mankind in a species of enslavement.

Within my own recollection unmarried white men could be sold for debt in the State of Connecticut; so that debt is a species of slavery, as commerce is a kind of commercial war. It is a war of interests, as all nations are using their highest arts to buy as cheap and sell as dear as they can.

Our Government can only regain its former prosperity as a nation by adopting a similar national policy to that which has made and protected the industries of France.

One of the causes that brought on the Revolutionary War, as will appear by the following statement, were the laws that were passed by England expressly to deprive her colonies of the right to manufacture for themselves.

"The first attempt at manufacture in the American colonies was followed by interference on the part of the British Legislature. . . . In 1710, the House of Commons declared that the erecting manufactories in the Colonies tended to lessen their dependence on Great Britain. In 1732, the exportation of hats from province to province, and the number of apprentices, was limited. . . . In 1750, the erection of any mill or engine for slitting or rolling iron was prohibited. . . . In 1765, the exportation of artisans from Great Britain was prohibited, under a heavy penalty. . . . In 1781, utensils required for the manufacture of wool or silk were prohibited. . . . In 1782, the prohibition was extended to artificers in printing calicoes, muslins, or linens, or in making implements used in their manufacture. . . . In

1785, the prohibition was extended to tools used in iron and steel manufacture, and to workmen so employed. . . . In 1799, it was so extended as to embrace even colliers.

"The war of the Revolution of our own country was brought on by a war of commercial interests. It was a war that showed a determination on the part of the mother country to keep her colonies entirely dependent on England for all forms of manufactured articles. Laws were enacted to prevent the colonies from manufacturing out of their own good raw materials things indispensable for their own use, and necessary to give employment to those who have nothing to sell but their own labor."

Washington, Franklin, Jefferson, and the Revolutionary fathers, were men who could see how utterly impossible it would be for the American people to *buy anything cheap from foreign countries that must be bought at the expense of leaving our own good raw materials unused and our own laborers unemployed.*

Our Constitution has declared that Congress shall have power to make all laws that shall be necessary and proper, to lay and collect taxes, duties, imports, excises, to pay the debts and provide for the common defence and the general welfare of these United States. Also "to borrow money on the credit of these United States."

It was by this constitutional power vested in Congress that all forms of Treasury notes were issued and used as so many dollars of legal money of the country. At the close of the war of the rebellion, our Government found itself encumbered with promises to pay that which it did not possess and could not command, only as the amount could be drawn from the people in some form of taxation. The promise to pay should never have been made. It should have been a promise to receive instead of a promise to pay tokens of debt which the Government had been compelled to pay out as money in its struggle for the nation's life. It was a currency that had proved itself, as President Grant had declared it to be, "the best money that our country had ever possessed, . . . that there was no more of it in circulation than what is required for the dullest business season of the year."

These facts being established by a condition of unsurpassed national prosperity that prevailed throughout our whole country at the close of a great and terrible war. After such a demonstration of the strength, wealth, and power of a nation, there was no good reason for acts of legislation avowedly to strengthen the credit of a nation that had carried on such a war *and obtained such a victory.*

What must the American people think when they come to know and understand that a governmental policy has been adopted that has taken from the people their currency that was furnished by the people without cost, and turned into such an oppressive debt as now burdens and paralyzes the industries of the country ?

The amount of currency so found in circulation at the close of the war should never have been allowed to increase or diminish, only as *per capita* with the increase of the inhabitants of the country.

Such a currency should have been made receivable for all forms of taxes, duties, and debts. That would have made our *national paper money* as much more valuable than gold in proportion as it would be more easily and cheaply handled in large sums.

Our national currency must be made receivable for all purposes throughout the country, and interconvertible with three per cent. Government bonds; it would then, like the consols of England, soon become an ever-strengthening bond of national union. Such a currency would have been worth more to the American people than all the gold mines that have ever been discovered on the continent of America.*

I hold our Government bound to give back to the people their small currency that was costing them nothing, and then call in the silver currency that has been put in its place at a cost of $31,738,400 paid for silver up to April 20, 1877. This silver should be immediately withdrawn, and used in the purchase of foreign bonds, thus saving for the American

---

* The following is a statement of the interest of money paid by the United States since the close of the war of the rebellion. The following statement shows that $1,422,057,577 has been paid in interest in 11¾ years :

Principal — Interest-bearing	$1,717,042,130
Non-interest-bearing	473,923,757
	$2,191,565,887
Interest due on above	33,092,616
	$2,224,658,503
Less cash in Treasury	154,290,886
Debt at May 1, 1877	$2,070,358,617
Debt at July 7, 1866	2,783,425,879
Reduction since July 1, 1866 (10 10–12 years)	$713,067,262

Since the close of the war, or from July 1, 1865, to April 1, 1877 (11¾ years), the interest on the public debt was $1,422,057,567, or $121,000,000 per annum !

The universal cry over the land is for employment. When well employed the people are well clothed, well fed, and well housed. The adjustment of the fiscal question—NOT *for one class*, but for the *masses*—must be made ere prosperity is ours. The recall from Europe of our gold bonds (by sale of commodities, placing them at low interest) and substituting greenbacks for national bank-notes, would remove grievous burdens, providing employment by stimulating our depressed industries.

Will President Hayes inaugurate this just policy, insuring general prosperity and spontaneous "resumption," or the par of paper with gold ?

The true remedy for national relief from the enslavement of debt, with its burden of taxation, is the substitution of greenbacks for national bank-notes.

The national banks have received since 1865 twenty-one millions of dollars interest on bonds deposited with the Government.

people an amount of interest, if compounded, that would pay the national debt several times in one hundred years, and at the same time give the country a more convenient currency, which would be more than paid for by the amount that would be worn out and lost by its use. If silver change is ever needed, it can be had with only the cost of coining it by the Government, as nearly all the silver produced in the country will go into coins whenever the Government will coin it without cost to its owners.

I find myself compelled to agree with Senator Jones where he says that "the present is the acceptable time to undo the unwitting and blundering work of 1873." . . . "We cannot, we dare not, avoid speedy action on the subject. Not only does reason, justice, and authority unite in urging us to retrace our steps, but the organic law commands us to do so, and the presence of *peril enjoins what the law commands.*"

I have ventured this long letter in the firm belief that the adoption of a permanent, unfluctuating national currency, as before stated, equal to the amount actually found in circulation at the close of the war, and *that amount should never be increased or diminished* only as per capita with the increase of the inhabitants of our country—such a measure of all internal values, with a revenue tariff of specific duties to be obtained from the smallest number of articles that will give the amount needed for an economical government—such a national policy would introduce prosperity once more into the trade, commerce, and finances of this country.

NOTE.—"*Expansion* versus *Contraction.*—The following statistics from the London *Economist* demonstrate the fact that the expansion of French Government legal tenders has kept pace with the accumulation of specie, and materially develops the home industries of that country:

"Of legal tenders in April, 1869, the circulation was 214 millions dollars, and in April, 1876, 494 millions, being an increase in seven years of 280 millions, or 130 per cent. !

"Of specie and bullion in December, 1869, the stock was 247 millions dollars, and in November, 1876, 432 millions, or an increase in seven years of 185 millions, or 75 per cent. !

"The striking prosperity of French industries under the above fiscal policy augurs strongly for an expansion equal to the amount found in circulation at the close of the war, and against a contraction."

Our Government has, from its origin, neglected to perform one of the most important duties enjoined on it by the Constitution, where it says that Congress shall have power not only to coin money but to regulate the value thereof. This can be and should have been done by an Act of Congress to regulate the value of money by fixing the amount that can be legally collected as interest for the use of money.

When such an Act has been provided to prevent extortionate demands for the use or interest on money, and when the law has been repealed that is now paralyzing the country with the terrible fact that some fifteen hundred millions of dollars now due from the people to the banks, with all the other debts that are to become due in 1879, *are by law* made payable in *gold*, then the way will be opened for a restoration of confidence and a permanent financial relief. The law contracting the currency is now taking from the people their legal money, costing the Government and the people nothing, and then converting this same currency into a national debt, for which the people are to be taxed for the next thirty years. It should never be forgotten that the first sixty millions of Treasury notes were issued and made " receivable in payments of duties on imports a lawful money and a legal tender."

The fact that the sixty millions then issued did continue receivable at the Treasury on a par with gold, when gold was selling at 285 in currency, this fact is proof positive that had the Government made all the greenbacks full legal tender, instead of sending them out partially demonetized and repudiated, they would never have fallen below par. It was the partial demonetization and the contraction of the currency that has so effectually destroyed confidence and dried up the sources of both production and consumption. The people are deprived of their currency which had for years formed the life blood of the trade and commerce of our country.

My efforts in all that I have written have been to call and fix the attention of the American people on those truths and principles so grandly set forth and declared in the Preamble to the Constitution, formed for us by the Fathers and founders of a Government intended to establish justice as the true and only sure means by which the general welfare of the American people can be substantially promoted.

Hoping and believing that your best efforts will be given to secure for our beloved country the blessings of a good Government,

I remain, yours, with great respect,

PETER COOPER.

NOTE.—The following quotations will show the monstrous absurdity of a national policy that would make all the industries of a nation to depend on an article like that of gold, the price of which no government or individual can control, as it bears one price to-day *and no man can tell what price will be offered for it to-morrow.*

To the above we append the following suggestions from John Earl Williams, President of the Metropolitan Bank of this city, in the same direction :

" I would suggest: That Congress assume, at once, the inherent sovereign prerogative of a government 'of the people, by the people, and for the people,' and exercise it, by furnishing all the inhabitants of the United States with a uniform national currency! Surely the people, and the people only, have a natural right to all the advantages, emolument, or income that may inure from the issue of either $1,000 bonds with interest, or $10 notes without, based on the faith and credit of the nation!

"This principle, simple, clear, and undeniable, ought to be recogn·zed as fundamental, and the only safe and proper basis on which may securely rest all the circulating medium of the country, for the sole benefit of all the people, and not, as now, for the profit of a class of stockholders, however deserving they may be in all other respects.

"To carry into effect this principle—to substitute United States notes for bank-notes—take away, as soon as practicable, and for ever, all circulation from banks.

"They would do a strictly legitimate business as banks of discount and deposit; knowing that whatever leads to the prosperity of the whole people must be beneficial to the banks; but leaving the right where it belongs, to the United States Government, to supply the whole circulating medium of the country.

"In this connection, we must remember that banks are the creatures of law. The laws which created them may, by virtue of rights reserved, be amended, altered, or repealed.

"To those who are disposed to complain of the change as a hardship, one is tempted to ask what natural right a dozen stockholders have to receive notes from Government to circulate that any other dozen men do not possess?

"One thing is certain, that the national debts can never be paid by a governmental policy that shrinks the currency, destroys values, paralyzes industry, enforces idleness, and brings wretchedness and ruin to the homes of millions of the American people. It is equally true that Americans can never buy anything cheap from foreign countries that must be bought at the expense of leaving our own good raw materials unused, and our own labor unemployed. It should be remembered that neither gold, silver, copper, nickel, or paper are money without the stamp of the Government upon it. The Constitution has made it the duty of Congress to coin the money of our country and regulate the value thereof, and fix a standard of weights and measures, as the only possible means by which commerce can be regulated between foreign nations and among the several States."

PETER COOPER.

THE DANGERS OF A WAR OF COMMERCE

AND THE NECESSITY OF A

TARIFF AND OF AN UNFLUCTUATING CURRENCY TO NATIONAL PROSPERITY.

By Peter Cooper.

"The experience of nearly eighty-one years has taught me that the greatest and most important question that now demands the consideration of the American people is, whether we, as a nation, are willing to know the truth, and let the truth make and maintain our freedom, or whether we have deliberately determined to follow the advice of men and nations that have a direct and an immediate interest to mislead and deceive us. For we may rest assured that all trade between foreign nations and our own is a kind of commercial war. It is a war of interests, as all nations are using their highest arts to buy as cheap and sell as dear as they can. All are trying to buy their raw materials in the cheapest market, and to sell their manufactured labor for the most that can be obtained for it. This they are doing by the use of all the arts, both fair and foul, that human ingenuity can devise.

"There has been nothing comparable with the evils that have and may result to nations from a war of commerce. Invasion of armies is attended with waste of property, destruction of life, and suspension of all fair exchange of the products of labor; but, with the return of peace, men can again combine their efforts, and in a few years all is as it had been before. Such, however, is not the case with the substitution of foreign trade, for the home commerce of the products of our own land and labor. Under the artful and alluring fascinations of the powers of foreign trade, association for mutual benefit dies away; intellect declines, and the life's blood of a nation slowly ebbs away, rendering recovery from day to day more difficult, and closing finally in the material and moral death of a nation.

"It can be shown that the wars of commercial interests are more insidious, and are more to be dreaded than wars of conquest. There is nothing in all history that admits of more complete demonstration than the fact that the wars of commercial interests, carried on by England alone, have led to and have caused a greater destruction of life and property, during the last seventy years, than has been occasioned by all the wars of conquest that have taken place in the civilized world during that period of time. It is now less than seventy-five years since a company, chartered by Great Britain, commenced a mercantile war on the people of Hindostan, a country with its then 150,000,000 of inhabitants, famed for manufacturing the finest quality of goods, and for being in possession of the riches of the East. History tells us that 'in no part of the world has there been seen a greater tendency to voluntary association for a mutual exchange of labor than once existed in Hindostan. . . . Each village had its distinct organization, under which the natives had lived from the earliest times down to a recent date. . . . Revolutions might occur, and dynasties might succeed each other; but, so long as his own little society was undisturbed, the simple Hindoo gave himself no concern about what might happen at the capital. . . . Though often over-taxed and plundered by invading armies, the country continued both rich and prosperous,' until an East India Company, chartered and sustained by the power of Great Britain, commenced a war of encroachments on the trade and commerce of that country. This war of commercial interests led to a war of conquest, which, after the battle of Plassey, had established British power in India. 'The country became filled with adventurers; men whose sole object was to accumulate fortunes, by any means, however foul,' as was shown by the indignant denunciation of Burke in the Parliament of Great Britain. Fox declared, in a speech on the East India Bill, that 'the country was laid waste with fire and sword, and the land once distinguished most above others by the cheerful face of fraternal government and protected labor, the chosen seat of cultivation and plenty, is now almost a dreary desert, covered with rushes and briers, jungles and wild beasts.' . . . The misgovernment of the English was carried to a point such as seemed *hardly compatible with the existence of society.* They forced the natives to buy dear and sell cheap.

" Macaulay says : ' The misgovernment was carried to such an extent as seemed hardly compatible with the existence of society. They forced the natives to buy dear and sell cheap. They insulted, with impunity, the tribunals, the police, and the fiscal authorities of the country. Enormous fortunes were thus rapidly accumulated at Calcutta, where 30,000,000 of human beings were reduced to the extremity of wretchedness. They had been accustomed to live under tyranny; but never tyranny like this. Under their old masters, they had one resource— when the evil became insupportable, the people pulled down the Government. But the English Government was not to be shaken off. That Government, oppressive as the most oppressive form of barbarian despotism, was strong with all the strength of civilization. It resembled the government of evil genii rather than the government of human tyrants. . . . Under the title of Zamindars, a landed aristocracy was created and held accountable for the collection of taxes.' Fullerton, a member of the Madras Council, says: ' Imagine the revenue leviable through 100,000 revenue officers ; collected or remitted at their discretion, according to the occupant's means of paying, whether from produce of the land or his separate property ; and in order to encourage every man to act as a spy on his neighbor and report his means of paying, that he may save himself from all extra demand ; imagine all the cultivators of a village liable at all times to a separate demand, in order to make up the failure of one or more individuals of the parish. Imagine collectors to every county, acting under the orders of a Board, on the avowed principle of destroying all competition for labor by a general equalization of assessments, seizing and sending back all runaways to each other. Lastly, imagine the collector, the sole magistrate or Justice of the Peace of the county; through the medium of whom alone, complaint of personal grievance suffered by the subject can reach the Superior Court. Imagine at the same time every subordinate officer employed in the collection of the land-revenue to be a police officer, vested with the power to confine, put in the stocks, and flay, any inhabitant within his range, on any charge, without oath of the accuser or sworn recorded evidence in the case.' . . . Under this state of things, 'the works constructed for irrigation have gone to ruin, and the richest lands have been abandoned.'

"Capt. Westmacot tells his readers that in many places the longest under British rule, there is the largest amount of depravity and crime. Campbell, one of the most distinguished of British poets, characterizes the course of their policy in India prophetically when he says:

> "'Foes of mankind!' her guardian spirits say,
> 'Revolving ages bring the bitter day,
> When heaven's unerring aim shall fall on you,
> And blood for blood these Indian plains bedew.'"

"'The immolations of an Indian Juggernaut,' says a recent writer, 'dwindle into insignificance before it, and yet to maintain this trade the towns and cities have been laid in ruins.' The middleman system of Ireland and of the West Indies was transplanted to those countries of the East, to which Macaulay declares that 'the English Government became as oppressive as the most oppressive form of barbarian despotism.' The poor Hindoo was not allowed to make salt from the waters of the ocean. Every form of tax and exaction was forced on that people in order to drive them to send all their cotton and wool to England (the great workshop of the world), to be converted and returned. Sir Robert Peel says: 'The effects in India exhibit themselves in such a ruin and distress that *no parallel can be found in the annals of commerce.*' The great city of Dacca, that only seventy years since contained 90,000 houses, and exported millions of pieces of the finest quality of goods, is now a mass of ruins. The same authority says: 'For the accomplishment of this work of destruction, the children of Lancashire, England, were employed fifteen to seventeen hours per day during the week, and until twelve o'clock on Sunday, cleaning and oiling machinery, for which they received two shillings and nine pence per week. The object was to underwork the poor Hindoo, and drive him from the markets of the world.' The pound of cotton, costing in India one cent, was passed through British looms, and sold to the Hindoo for from forty to sixty cents. 'Thus England was enriched, as India became impoverished. Step by step, British power was extended, and everywhere was adopted the Hindoo principle *that the sovereign, as proprietor of the soil, was entitled to half of the gross produce.*' While these exorbitant local taxes were expended among its own people, the burden could be borne; when these taxes were drawn from the people and expended on absentee landlords, the burden brought desolation and premature death to millions of the people of that country. History tells us that one-half of the labor of that people ran to waste for the want of employment.

"The exactions of British power in China, made to force the sale of opium in that country, are stated to cause the death annually of 500,000 of the Chinese people, besides a tax of nearly $20,000,000. Campbell says, 'the immolations of an Indian Juggernaut dwindle into insignificance before it.' The ruin of Portugal was effected by the Government having been induced to adopt a British commercial policy that broke up the harmony of the agricultural and mechanical interests— interests that had for so long a time made Portugal so rich and prosperous. 'It is less than two hundred years since the merchants of London *petitioned their Government to restrain the manufacture of cloth in Ireland*.' Of all the 1,700,000 slaves imported into the British West India Islands, only 660,000 were found living on the day of emancipation. This was the result of a war of commerce. The planters on those islands had been deprived by law of all right 'to refine their own sugar, or to introduce a spindle or a loom, or to mine coal, or to smelt their own copper,' thus depriving the people of the islands of all power of association, and exchange of labor and harmony of interests, without which ruin falls to the lot of every community. The British policy that was forced on the Island of Jamaica alone cost the lives of hundreds of thousands of men, in order that a few absentee owners might live in splendor on the Island of England. The policy of forcing the whole labor of a community into the single pursuit of making sugar effectually prevented the growth of towns and schools, and impoverished the people and the land. All communities require the families of the blacksmith, the carpenter, mason, and of other tradesmen, to consume a large part of the agricultural product of the soil, to secure them prosperity, and to enable them to leave offal to enrich the land that feeds them. 'On the Island of Jamaica, with a population of 320,000 black laborers, and with inexhaustible supplies of timber, that island has been without a single saw-mill up to 1860.' Out of the amount paid to the British Government by the people thirty years since for the products of its 320,000 black laborers, the Home Government took no less than $18,000,000, or almost $60 per head, and this merely for superintending the exchanges. The negroes imported into Jamaica were no more barbarian than those brought to Virginia and North Carolina; yet, while each of the negroes imported into the latter States is represented by seven of his descendants, the British Islands present but two for every five they have received. But a century since, Portugal and the West Indies were England's best customers. What are they now? All impoverished by a policy that has broken up their own home commerce, and has subjected their countries to the heaviest kind of tax— the tax of transporting their heavy products to great distances, to be exchanged for the light products of other countries.

"'The first attempt at manufacture in the American Colonies was followed by interference on the part of the British Legislature. . . . In 1710, the House of Commons declared that the erecting manufactories in the Colonies tended to lessen their dependence on Great

Britain.' 'In 1732 the exportation of hats from province to province and the number of apprentices was limited. . . . In 1750, the erection of any mill or engine for slitting or rolling iron was prohibited. . . In 1765, the exportation of artisans from Great Britain was prohibited, under a heavy penalty. . . . In 1781, utensils required for the manufacture of wool or silk were prohibited. . . . In 1782, the prohibition was extended to artificers in printing calicoes, muslins, or linens, or in making implements used in their manufacture. . . . In 1785, the prohibition was extended to tools used in iron and steel manufacture, and to workmen so employed. . . . In·1799, it was so extended as to embrace even colliers.'

" The war of the Revolution of our country was brought on by a war of commercial interests. It was a war that showed a determination on the part of the mother-country to keep her colonies entirely dependent on England for all forms of manufactured articles. Laws were enacted to prevent the colonies from manufacturing out of their own good raw materials things indispensable for their own use, and necessary to give employment to those who have nothing to sell but their own labor. The war of the Revolution was a war of resistance to a war of commerce then being forced by the mother-country on the colonies. Our conquest of a country did not deliver us from the consummate power of highly-educated British diplomats, whose business it has always been to find the weak places in surrounding governments, and to so control the legislation of those countries as to make them tributary to the wealth and power of Great Britain. These diplomats, after having secured for their own manufacturing interests more perfect protection and more perfect mechanical powers than any other nation possessed, have enabled their Government to gain greater advantages by their war of commerce on our own country than they could have gained if the colonies had remained entirely under their own control. Such has been the consummate ability that foreign diplomacy has been able to exert in a war of commerce that has brought our country in debt to foreign Governments to an amount the interest on which is now equivalent to a large proportion of the agricultural export of the country. This state of things must continue or grow worse, unless our Government will raise its whole revenue out of duties on imports, and relieve the country from all forms of direct taxation, and by that means encourage the application of knowledge, economy, and labor, in a course of efforts to supply our own wants by our own industry, out of our own good raw materials, that can be put into useful forms with as small an expense of human labor here as in any other part of the world. Thus it will enable the country to win back its independence of foreign debt by paying it off as fast as the amount can be raised from the duties on imports.

" Our Government can only hold its power as a free system by avoiding in future all special, partial, or class legislation, and by the enactment of only such general laws as are necessary and indispensable to establish justice. Justice can only be established ' and the general welfare promoted ' by the Government holding an entire control over all that is allowed or intended to measure or weigh the different forms and values of labor in its course of exchange from one person to another Hence the absolute necessity for the establishment of a just and unyielding system of money, weights, and measures. This is indispensable to facilitate the business of the country. If paper is to be coined into money the amount should be limited and so regulated that the sum could only be increased in regular proportion with the natural increase of the inhabitants of the country. All Government paper should be a legal tender in the payment of all private debts that were contracted during the time that paper is allowed to circulate as money. All persons should have the privilege of paying duties on imports, and also all contracts to pay gold, by adding to the amount in legal tenders a sum sufficient to be equal to the average premium that gold had sold for during the month preceding the maturing of the contract—the Government to advertise the rate of premium on the 1st of every month.

"The people of our country should never forget that one of the great causes that led to the American Revolution was the determination on the part of Great Britain to force its manufactures on the colonies, to be paid for by sending raw materials to England; thus keeping them dependent by preventing them from manufacturing for themselves. This policy of England has drawn to its little island the wealth of every country that has allowed itself to become the subject of its policy and power. It is still trying to persuade the people of this country to run their ploughs in competition with the mighty machines in England, where a single engine is doing the work of a thousand horses. To see the folly of yielding to a British policy, we have only to look at the effects produced on our country during the war with England. At that time, when our foreign trade was cut off, labor was in demand and money abundant; furnaces and mills were built, and all actively employed; wages were high, and our national debt small. Four years later, our country was persuaded to yield to a British policy of Free Trade. At once all was changed; mills and furnaces were stopped, labor went begging, our poorhouses were filled, the prices of land declined, money became scarce, and interest high; the rich who held mortgages became richer, and the poor and those who were in debt, were ruined. At that time the American farmer had no foreign or home market for the surplus product of the country. Complaints grew and increased until things grew so bad that in 1828 our Government found it necessary to adopt what I call a true American system—a system of Free Trade—a trade that extended to all parts of our own country in all articles that are the product of our own soil or of American labor. By this system duties were laid on imports that soon gave new life and energy to the trade and business of the country. The public debt was soon paid off, and prosperity became universal.

"By degrees, between 1834 and 1842, the tariff was again repealed by the influence of southern and pro-slavery politicians, whose whole wealth was invested in cotton and slaves. The mills were again stopped, furnaces closed, lands fallen to half-price, the sheriff at work, States repudiating their debts, the Treasury unable to borrow at home or abroad, and bankrupt laws passed by Congress. In 1842, the true

American System was again tried; and in less than five years the production of iron alone rose from 200,000 tons to 800,000 tons. Prosperity was again universal, mines were opened, mills were built, and money plenty, and the public and private revenues greater than ever. Once more, in 1846, the British policy of Free Trade was adopted·by repealing our tariff, and, notwithstanding the discovery of gold in California, money was as high as ever. British iron came in and gold went out. In 1857, the culmination was reached, and a crisis came on. The Treasury was again nearly bankrupt. In three years, emigration fell below the point of twenty-eight years before, and our own exports fell off to a mere nothing. Such have been the effects of yielding to a policy recommended by men and nations having interests to serve that are at war with all the best interests of our own country.

"A war of commercial interests is not peculiar to England alone. It has been the habit of all trading nations since 'naught said the buyer.' They will all continue to buy in the cheapest market and sell in the dearest as long as men do not love their neighbors as they do themselves. There are thousands of those now engaged in foreign trade whose fortunes depend on filling the country with foreign goods. There are other thousands who are holders of mortgages, who hope to buy in the property for the face of their mortgages, or for half its present value. And that they *will do as soon as they can induce our Government to try another experiment in what they call free trade.* The policy of these persons, who are all clamorous for free trade, would deprive millions of men of their means of living by mechanical employments, and drive them into competition with the farming and agricultural interests of the country, making the mechanics competitors of the farmers; instead of consuming, as they now do, ten times as much of the agricultural product of the country as is now sold in all Europe.

"It would be as unwise for our country in time of war to govern the movements of armies by the advice of our enemy as it would be for our Government to allow our national policy to be controlled by the advice of the trading nations of Europe, who will always consult their own interests, entirely independent of any interests of ours. It is well to remember that there is nothing that can be said to be purchased cheap of foreign countries that must be bought *at the expense of leaving our own labor unemployed, and our own good raw materials unused.* I advocate the cause of our manufacturing interests, because they secure to the farmer his surest and best market for the agricultural product of the country, and because experience has demonstrated the fact that the surest way to maintain our independence, and cheapen goods to the consumer, is to foster the home productions of our country, and give diversified employment to our people. And I advocate an American system, because I desire the political power and the financial honor of the nation to be maintained and vindicated before the world. This can be most effectually accomplished by making ourselves independent as far as our own soil and climate and good raw materials will enable us to produce the articles we need; and this they do with as small an expense of labor as it would require to produce the same articles in any other part of the world. I advocate a policy that will maintain the

National Government and pay the nation's debt out of duties on imports. The heaviest duties should be laid on all articles of luxury, and the lightest duties on all articles that will aid in securing a diversified employment to our people.

"There is nothing else that our Government can do that will so effectually stimulate and develop all the best energies of a free people as will the adoption of a *just, uniform, and unyielding system of money, weights, and measures.* It is greatly to be regretted that our Government failed in its very commencement to perform the most important duty enjoined by the Constitution. They should never have allowed the individual States to issue paper money that *was to all intent bills of credit.* It has been the inflation of irredeemable paper money that has so raised the price of all property and labor that we now tempt the world to sell us everything, and we have made everything with us too dear to sell with profit in return. Free Trade with foreign nations *must,* where all things have been made unequal by the use of paper money, prove in the future, as it has in the past, a delusion and a snare. It must in the future, as it has in the past, bring panic, pressure, and ruin, to untold thousands made bankrupt by the change of value in all kinds of property. This must be the result of leaving our own labor unemployed and our own good raw materials unused."

But it should ever be borne in mind that besides the great disadvantage which always results to a nation by depending abroad for the supply of its wants, for any product of the soil, or of manufacture, which can as well, if encouraged, be produced at home, we have to encounter also "*a drain of specie,*" which, if it be our only money and legal tender, subjects the value of the paper, *based on coin,* to great fluctuations in value, owing to this drain which such a commerce brings on the country, and thus becomes a source of incalculable loss and misfortune to the country liable to such a drain of its money. But a *national paper currency of our own* (greenbacks), made a perfect legal tender, and always interconvertible into bonds, would be a complete protection against a drain of our money, and leave our gold and silver, as the rest of our productions, to pay all "balances of trade." The "American policy" is, therefore, a Tariff, with a "*domestic, unexportable, and well-founded currency.*"   EDITOR.

LABOR PROSPERITY IN ENGLAND EIGHTEEN YEARS—FROM 1797 TO 1815.

Extract from MARVIN WARREN'S Work on American Labor.

Sir Archibald Alison, author of the *History of Modern Europe,* says: "The next eighteen years of the war, from 1797 to 1815, were, as all the world knows, the most glorious, and taken as a whole, the most prosperous which Great Britain had ever known. Ushered in by a combination of circumstances the most calamitous, both with reference to external security and internal industry, it terminated in a blaze of glory and flood of prosperity which have never since the beginning of the world descended upon any nation. Prosperity universal and unheard of pervaded every part of the empire. Our colonial possessions encircled the earth; the whole West India Islands had fallen into our hands; an empire of sixty millions of men in Hindoostan acknowledged our rule; Java was added to our Eastern possessions; and the flag of France had disappeared from every station beyond the sea. Agriculture, commerce, and manufactures at home had increased in an unparalleled ratio; the landed proprietors were in affluence; wealth to an unheard of extent had been created among the farmers; the soil, daily increasing in fertility and breadth of cultivated lands, had become almost adequate to the maintenance of a rapidly increasing population; our exports, imports, and tonnage had more than doubled since the war began."

What caused this prosperity? Exactly the same thing in kind that causes the present French prosperity. This eighteen years of English prosperity commenced in 1797, when the Bank of England was authorized by the Government to suspend specie payment, and continued just so long as it was not insisted upon by any party that the bank should be required to pay specie, and ceased immediately as soon as that requirement was seriously urged. The money of England during that eighteen years was irredeemable paper money; it was rag baby in its nature. The very kind of money that the ministers of finance in our country tell us is a sore evil to have. True, like our present greenback money, it was inferior to the French paper money, because it was not a full legal tender for all debts in the country. Of course, then, it depreciated some in value as compared to gold, and did not have that full and complete beneficial effect, in dispensing its benefits to all interest and to everybody, as it otherwise would, and as the French money does. But like the French money in one respect it was not redeemable in specie on demand, and hence it could be and was issued in quantities for the most part to adapt itself to the necessities of labor and business. Take notice, American laborers, that this period of English prosperity lasted just the eighteen years of time that the money of England was not disturbed by redeemability in specie, nor seriously threatened so to be, and not any longer. So that English experience and French experience as to what causes prosperity accord one with the other, and they both are to the effect that prosperity comes at once, upon the liberation of the money or currency of the country from being redeemed in specie, and then issued in quantities suited to put the labor of the country all into active and profitable employment.

And take notice, also, just what kind of prosperity that was. It was the prosperity of labor; all honest, useful labor. It was "prosperity universal and unheard of," and it "pervaded in every part of the empire." "Agriculture, commerce, and manufactures at home had increased in an unparalleled ratio." And take notice, American farmers, the landed proprietors were in affluence, and wealth to an unheard of extent had been created among the farmers.

And I say this, also, that there was not in that English prosperity anything at all savoring of fiction, or wanting of substantiality. It was built on labor, and the labor stimulated by honest principles of finance that simply rewarded the laborer instead of robbing him. If those principles had been followed up and perfected, and kept alive in the laws of the country, instead of being supplanted by fraud and fiction, as they afterward were, that prosperity would have lasted to this day, and would last as much longer as the true principles might be preserved. And so in our own country, we cannot only have that prosperity, but we can establish it upon principles that shall make it enduring, and that is the business of the true men of this generation.

Why was it that just in that eighteen years of war England authorized her national banking institution to suspend specie payments and issue money in quantities suited to the industrial and commercial wants and prosperity? It was because Napoleon was then pressing her by his military power, and the very existence of the Government and nation itself required all the resources of the nation to be brought into active use for its defence, suspending for the time being the avaricious gains of the moneyed nobility. As stated above by the historian, this eighteen years was "ushered in by a combination of circumstances the most calamitous, both with reference to external security and internal industry." Think of it. All this prosperity came, not by favored circumstances, but in spite of circumstances, external and internal, the most calamitous; all simply through the power of honesty and truth, in the money of the country.

But in 1815, the war closed by the capture of Napoleon at Waterloo. The scourge of war now being removed, it seems to have been thought that the country could endure without entire destruction a scourge far worse than the war; and the Shylocks, with Sir Robert Peel at their head, or as an associate, began to insist seriously upon a law for resumption of specie payments. And then what took place?

Let Thomas Doubleday, in his financial, monetary and statistical history of England, tell what took place. He says: "Prices fell on a sudden to a ruinous extent—banks broke—wages fell with prices of manufactures; and before the year 1816 had come to a close, panic, bankruptcy, riot, and disaffection had spread through the land. Vast bodies of starving and discontended artisans now congregated together and demanded reform of the Parliament. The discontents, as usual, the Government put down by an armed force. As the memorable first of May, 1823, drew near, the country bankers, as well as the Bank of England, naturally prepared themselves by a gradual narrowing of their circulation for the dreaded hour of gold and silver payments on demand. . . . . The distress, ruin and bankruptcy which now took place were universal, affecting both the great interests of land and trade."

Peel and his Shylock backers pressed the matter of the specie resumption law, and it was passed in 1819, requiring by its terms, specie payments to commence May 1, 1823—four years. Between the years 1815 and 1825, inclusive, by the specie resumption law, and by the loss of confidence growing out of its pendency, more than four-fifths of the landowners of England lost their possessions. The number of land-owners was reduced from 160,000 to 30,000. The very farmers that had accumulated wealth to an unheard of extent in the eighteen years of suspension, now became bankrupt and penniless.

Wendell Phillips, in a letter to the New York Legal Tender Club, dated August 23, 1875, though slightly inaccurate in two or three historical dates and some other forms of expression, draws a faithful sketch of this English resumption, as compared to our own now in progress but not completed. The following is an extract of the letter :

" History is repeating itself. England never knew more prosperous years than from 1800 to 1820, during which she had neither gold nor wished to have it, nor promised to pay gold to any one whatever. All that while she extended and contracted her currency without any regard whatever to gold. Her enormous trade and expenditures were all paper, resting on credit and nothing else. We had similar prosperity during the war, and after on the same terms. In 1820, England, listening to theorists, tried to put this new wine into old bottles, and dragged her business back to methods a century old—to specie. Bankruptcy, the very history of which makes the blood cold to-day, blighted the empire. It took half a generation to recover from the mistake. No man can to-day begin to show that such suffering was necessary, that it achieved any good, or that it effected any change which could not have been as well made without it."

The object was not to have the paper currency redeemed in specie ; there was really no desire or expectation of that ; but simply that the paper money be driven from circulation, by making this impossible requirement of specie payment in respect to it, thus leaving but very little currency in circulation of any kind, and forcing down prices of labor and property, real estate especially, to almost nothing, rendering debtors unable to pay their debts, that their estates might be bought in at forced sales, or voluntary to prevent the forced, at prices ruinous, and quite likely still leaving them in debt and without means to pay.

The scheme worked like a charm. By it under the forms and sanction of law, the property of the English people was gathered up in vast sweeping accumulations, and handed over to the nobility, and thus was the genius of the British society, its distinction of nobility and vassalage, restored intact.

The specie resumption law of this country, passed in January, 1875, is in substance and design a copy of the British law of 1819, above mentioned. Bear in mind the excuse is to redeem the paper currency in specie, the real object is to drive from circulation the currency of the country, reduce prices, and so rob the debtor class.

But let us look at the matter. What will the national bank-notes be redeemable in when the greenbacks are withdrawn and burned up? The bank-notes must be redeemable in something, else they will be worthless, for they are not a legal tender for debt, as the greenback money is. At present the bank-notes are redeemable in legal tender greenbacks, and that makes them good. But the greenbacks withdrawn and burned up, and then what? Why, the bank-notes must then be redeemable in specie of course, as the resumption law provides. And where will the banks get the specie to redeem with? Some of the strongest of them will be able to get it, and continue their business But it looks to us that the bank-note circulation will be contracted instead of enlarged under the operation of this specie resumption law. Contraction has been the effect of it so far, and we have every reason to believe it will be more and more so up to the time of resumption. The requirement to redeem in specie causes this. That was the effect in England, as shown in the foregoing extract from Doubleday's History.

The contraction under our specie resumption law up to November 1, 1876, was $30,710,732 of national bank-notes, and $14,464,284 of greenbacks, besides $20,910,946 more of greenbacks deposited in the treasury of the United States for the retirement of national bank-notes, making a total contraction of the currency of $66,085,962 up to the date mentioned, and the contraction and destroying of the greenback money is still going on.

But when this contraction has gone on for a certain time and instead of a diffused and large credit pervading the country, we have all the loanable capital concentrated in the great money centres, and controlled by the banks, then *expansion* of credits will be the order of the day. Bank credit will be thrown out in unlimited quantity, in the shape of bank-notes, ostensibly redeemable in specie, but really not; but all *secured* as loans on the property of the borrower. Then the banks and the money lenders have only to *contract* these loans, and the securities being suddenly thrown upon the market, sweeps the property of the many into the hands of the few. This is the game of all banking.

We purpose not to be an alarmist, and believe we are not. We think we have no motive or desire whatever to create misapprehension, or groundless fear or unjust distrust of the integrity or capacity of those in authority. But if this greenback money, constituting as it now does more than half of the currency of the country, be withdrawn from circulation by the first of January, 1879, the time fixed for resumption, there will be no enlargement of the bank-note circulation to take its place, or at least a very inadequate one, and probably a contraction instead, and at that time there will be precipitated upon the people of this country a financial disaster and loss of estates, like unto and probably equal to that which was brought upon the English people in 1823, when more than four-fifths of the land-owners of that country were robbed of their possessions. All our principal finance laws passed in the last eleven years seem to us framed with a direct reference to a grand future crisis of that kind, to be brought about by contraction of the currency. We do not believe there has been a single annual report of our Secretary of the Treasury in all that eleven years that did not contain one or more recommendations, equally monstrous with that one just quoted from the last report, seeming to us to ignore the plainest dictates of common reason, common justice, and practical experience, and aiming for a future crisis such as above mentioned.

I now ask the reader to again peruse carefully the progress of the English crisis from its beginning, in 1815, to its culmination, in 1823, the time of resumption, as given in the above extract from Doubleday's History, and compare therewith, as far as we have progressed, our own experience, embracing the last eleven years of our history, again inspecting withal the table of bankruptcies. It will be found that we are travelling the same road exactly, and unless our people demand a halt, or restrain the Government by popular demands, we are destined to the same end. The only difference is, that the game here has to proceed slower and more cautiously, more shifts and devices are needed, and more newspaper aid has to be employed here to befog the people than was required in England, because history throws more light on the subject now than it did then, and because the people here have more to do in the cause of Government than they had in England; and moreover, by reason of our greater natural resources, our country is able, without total and immediate ruin, to endure a greater amount of robbery. I do not believe there was ever such a horrid system of usury practised amongst men as preys upon this country at this very time.

The crisis proceeds here as it did in England, with increasing bankruptcy of business firms, throwing laborers more and more out of employment. According to reliable statistics, failures in bankruptcy in this country have had a general increase for the last eleven years, being nineteen times as much in 1876 as in 1865. And every increase of bankruptcy has been marked by an increase of pauperism, suffering, death from destitution, disaffection, political and governmental corruption, and a failing of the confidence of our own people in our own republican institutions.

Specie basis or specie payments should be something of great value to cost so much suffering. What is it, therefore, and what is it for? This specie basis, or specie payment, is a something written down in the books of British science, and from thence copied into ours. Specie is a something that a very few wealthy men, of almost any country, can buy up and hold at will, substantially the entire stock in that country, as is done now in the United States. This being done, then if there be no law for any legal tender paper money in the country, but all the money, in order to be good, must be either specie or redeemable in specie, these few men will hold entire control of the money of the country, and can control all business and prices, and virtually own nearly everything in the country sooner or later, as always is done where this specie basis fraud exists.

Again, this same specie is good to make watch cases, watch chains, and gold and silver dishes of, and to work into an innumerable variety of ornaments for persons, male and female, and otherwise to gratify the whims, vanity, and pomp of the wealthy classes. And to what extent it may be required for this purpose in any one country depends upon the changes of fashion and the ability of men to indulge in it, either of which is unstable as the waves of the sea. Likewise in times of war, danger, or financial uncertainty, this specie is good to hoard up, and is hoarded by men who are able, from motives of both security and speculation.

And besides these things occurring within the country, the like casualties all over the world, together with the uncertainty of the yield of the mines, and the ever-varying laws of the different countries in monetizing and demonetizing gold and silver and other materials, make the presence and availability of specie, either for money or the basis of currency, one of the most unreliable things in this unreliable world.

Yet British science calls this most fickle commodity the most reliable for a money basis. This policy will do for the British nobility as a most excellent fiction by which to turn systematically to themselves the earning of the British laborers, as is constantly done in that country. It may also do for American politicians or office-seekers (who, as we are aware, are excusable if they have no ideas of their own) to prate about, so as to please the money-dealers and get their money support. But an American farmer, who is entitled to vote, and has a farm that he desires to keep and not have filched from him, and every other person identified with the labor interests of the country, should consult his own common reason and his practical observation of things, and not lay aside either of these to be misled and ensnared by British fiction and clap-trap.

To know anything about this subject of money it is necessary to pause right here and consider definitely what specie basis or specie payments mean. Most people think they do understand it, and yet do not exactly. Very many think that because we, the greenback men, oppose specie basis we oppose specie money. This is furtherest possible from the truth. We do not object to specie money. The greenback principles, if thoroughly carried out, will make specie abundant in the country. Nor do we very seriously object to having our paper money promise to be redeemed in specie. The dependence on redemption in specie as an exclusive basis, so called—this is what we do object to most strenuously, and having the value of currency depend in the least degree upon its being so redeemed in specie. That is, the paper currency, whether so redeemed or not, should be a full legal tender for all debts throughout the country, the same as specie, so as to keep it par with specie in value. Owing to the fickle nature of specie there is, in fact, no such thing as specie basis for the currency of any commercial nation. Specie basis means no basis at all, but the absolute power of a few men to decide in their own interests how much currency the people shall have for business, or whether any at all or not, with power to change the amount to suit their own speculative purposes.

To illustrate still more completely the real nature of this specie basis idea, take, for example, our own country, the United States. Now, any one year of prosperous business throughout this country would be attended always by two things : one is the activity of its money passing from hand to hand, the other is growth. In other words, if we have a single year of active, healthy business, we are ready the next year to do a still greater business. Business grows with its growth. Growth of business requires a corresponding growth in the quantity of money, just exactly as a tree that grows vigorously one year by the nourishment of the earth and air, received through the sap, requires a greater quantity of that sap the next year to continue the growth and health of the tree. Hence we see, in the Creator's order of things, as a tree grows larger its roots, fibres, and foliage reach forth deeper and higher and broader, that they may gather and transmit the necessary increase of sap and nourishment to the whole tree. Circumscribe those roots and fibres, or otherwise withhold the necessary increase of sap required by nature, and you dwarf the tree or kill it.

Precisely so it is with nations. Prosperity, if we have any, is attended with growth, and a necessity for an increase of money. Withhold the increase of money and you will dwarf the nation, or kill it, and murder the inhabitants. Under a specie basis order of things what has the supply of specie to do with the wants of the nation for more or less money. Is it anywhere revealed to us that mines and jobbers will always give forth a supply just suited to the business necessities? Nay, verily. But in proportion as you attempt to actually base the currency on specie will the jobbers grasp the specie and keep it out of legitimate business. Thus you limit the money of the country by an arbitrary, irresponsible power, that feels no sympathy with the money wants of the nation. The theory, therefore, of basing the money of a country upon specie, the most liable of all materials to be snatched away for luxury, vanity, and speculation, and all the more sure to be so snatched away as the more we attempt actually to base money upon it, is a diabolical idea, a wholesale, murderous conception, and contrary to the Creator's order of things. To say that such materials, gold or silver, or both together, constitute the best basis for currency, is as contrary to the truth as to say that a brothel is the best place to preserve chastity, or that the taking of strong drink is the best way to keep temperate, or that a deep-sounding bed of quick-sand is the best foundation for a house.

England herself does not in reality base her currency on specie, nor could she without bringing all business to a dead stop in a very short time. She just mixes enough of this specie basis fiction in her finances to continually or periodically divest the laboring classes of their earnings for the benefit of the nobility. But for the real basis of value to her currency, she makes the notes of the Bank of England, as well as her coins, a full legal tender for the payment of debts, but not the notes of the other banks. From this we see that even in England specie basis is a mere fiction, a false pretence.

We have already seen what a terrible siege of robbery, destitution, suffering, and death the Government of England made its people pass through from 1815 to 1823, to reach specie basis, or specie payments, the pretended haven of rest and happiness. And what was the result? The following statement being condensed from an article in the St. Louis *Commercial* of March 23, 1876, shows what that specie payment bliss amounted to when obtained:

"At the time of Napoleon's defeat at Waterloo, in 1815, the Bank of England and the country banks had an issue of $270,000,000. The cry of resumption being raised, the banks set about a sharp contraction of both their issues and their discounts. Between 1815 and 1823, they reduced the volume of their issue 33 per cent.

"The crisis was at its height from the 12th to the 17th of December, 1825. Up to the night of the 14th the Bank of England had restricted its issues; but at that time, becoming sensible of its error, it resolved to make common cause with the country, and issued circulating notes to the amount of $25,000,000. This policy was crowned with the most complete success. The panic was stayed almost instantly. Credit was revived, and a needless and protracted period of suffering was averted. This remedy consisted in a profuse issue of irredeemable paper money to the amount of $25,000,000.

"Similar but less disastrous panics happened in 1836 and 1839, and from then to 1843 general commercial stagnation prevailed throughout England.

"In 1844, Peel's restriction act was passed by Parliament, forbidding the bank to issue beyond 14,000,000 pounds sterling on the Government stocks, except she has the gold in her vaults, pound for pound.

"Three years after this act was passed, in 1847, the next panic ensued. The extreme pressure began September 23d and continued until October 23d, when the terrible game was played out. The Queen's Government ordering the act suspended and the currency expanded, two millions of dollars, with the assurance that plenty more could be had, cured this panic instanter.

"In 1857 the most unexpected and disastrous crisis they had ever experienced swept across to them from our shores. To stop this panic the bank act was suspended again, and the currency—paper money—was expanded nearly $34,000,000, in excess of the limit, which then stood at nearly 15,000,000 pounds.

"In 1866, they had it again. The Chancellor of the Exchequer said the excitement was without parallel. On the evening of this black Friday, the ministry advised the suspension of the bank act, which was done the next morning, and in the course of five days $60,000,000 of paper money issued to the entire relief of business and restoration of confidence."

From the above it will be seen what a beautiful thing this forced specie payment was when reached through the horrible robbery of the English people in 1823. After it was reached it was maintained with increasing suffering and misery for two years and seven months, and then December 17, 1825, a suspension had to take place, and $25,000,000 of irredeemable paper money had to be issued to stay the wretchedness. And again another author, Hon. Isaac Buchanan, says: "England seems to the world to have survived the process of a return to specie payment, although how she has done so, if gone into in detail, would be the saddest and most harrowing record of human suffering. . . . At the end of thirty years (in 1839) the revenue, or in other words the property of the country, got fairly broken down, under the insidious operations of the British money system." Further the honorable gentleman says that, in the 1847 panic, thousands died of starvation in the cellars of the manufacturing and seaport towns of Great Britain.

Such are the effects of specie basis, or specie payments, so called, a thing that the English Government pretended to think of such great value, and so desirable, as that, in order to reach it, she dragged her people from a condition of "prosperity universal and then unheard of," through eight years of unheard-of bankruptcy, starvation, and misery, and then, when reached, the result was a continuation of the same horrors, until relieved again in two years and seven months by a temporary return to suspension of specie payments and the issue of irredeemable paper money. And then again, after twenty years more of miserable existence on the part of the labor of the country, we find the laborers dying by thousands, of starvation, in the cellars of the manufacturing and seaport towns. And still these scenes have been followed by successive horrors of a similar kind at intervals ever since, relieved in every instance by a *return to suspension and an issue of irredeemable paper money.*

And still further, as late as 1875, we find the Chamber of Commerce of the British kingdom unanimously adopted a resolution praying the Chancellor of Exchequer to appoint a commission to inquire, amongst other things, "into the constitution and actual management of the Bank of France, as compared with the constitution and actual management of the Bank of England; as to the points of difference in the constitution and actual management of those banks respectively, to which may be attributed the crisis and panics which occur periodically in the English money market, and do *not occur in the French money market at all.*"

Now, it is to be borne in mind that there has been no specie payments in France since 1870, or at least no law yet in force requiring it; and yet the paper money of that country, unlike that of England, is all a full legal tender, and all the time substantially par with gold. This is the one essential point of difference between the two systems of money of those two countries, the French paper currency, or money, is a full legal tender for the payment of all debts, public and private, within the realm, and can, therefore, issue continually, and does issue, in sufficient quantities for the business of the country, without any depreciation of value. Whilst in England, the bills of none of the banks, except the Bank of England, are a general legal tender for debt, but depend for their value on being redeemed in specie, or in the Bank of England bills; whilst the bills of the Bank of England, although a legal tender, are limited usually to such amount as can be redeemed in specie. That is, in short, the English paper money is, to some extent at least, specie basis money, whilst that of France is irredeemable, rag-baby stuff, essentially such as England had in time of her great prosperity, and yet such as the prevailing authorities of this country and England call a pernicious evil, but which the commercial or mercantile interests of England are longing to have established in opposition to the specie basis fiction of the money craft of that country.

Note.—The foreign balance of trade, in our favor at present, is, in this instance, not the result of prosperity at home, but of lack of employment and poverty among our people. Our bankruptcies and bankrupt sales being of greater number than any former year, and laborers more unemployed than ever, would seem to indicate that we have not been producing more, but have been selling abroad cheap, and buying less from abroad, because of increased poverty among laborers. That is, we sold cheap abroad because our own people were too much unemployed and poor to buy and use what were to them the necessaries of life and of business. And our own factories, to a very large extent, are unable to be run at all, only because, having changed hands, the present owners got them almost for nothing, and are able to get work-hands on the same scale of prices. What a triumph is this of governmental political economy! The real test of prosperity is, whether or not labor has been employed and well paid. And labor was never so much unemployed, and never so poorly paid in any one previous year as in 1876, showing a constant decline in our industrial and financial condition, despite of constant prediction tc the contrary by our Government functionaries and their Shylock admirers.

And, furthermore, the withdrawal of the greenback money from circulation, as recommended by our Secretary of the Treasury, and President Grant, also, will itself bring greatly increased prostration of labor and business, and turn the flow of specie away from us, provided we shall then have any to flow away.

When Mr. Chase was Secretary of the Treasury, in time of the war, and before the commencement of this eleven years of decline, he desired authority from Congress to receive deposits of money in the Treasury from our people, payable back on ten days' notice in our own lawful paper money, with interest at five per cent. This would have been on the like principle of the interconvertible bond, now urged by the greenback advocates. Had the plan of Mr. Chase been carried out, it would have enabled our Government to obtain constant credit among our own business men to the amount of several hundred millions of dollars, much to the benefit of the men themselves, and the saving of gold bonds being issued to foreigners. But Congress was full of bankers, as it always is, and they wanted these private deposits to bank on themselves; for which reason the Secretary was permitted to receive only one hundred millions in this way, which was eagerly deposited.

One Secretary of the Treasury under President Grant's administration, by long-continued effort, funded five hundred millions of our national debt in gold bonds and sold them in the foreign market, when, had our people been provided with legal tender paper money, so as to have kept our labor employed at home, after the French manner, we could have paid off the whole five hundred millions in less time than the Secretary was funding it. The policy seems to be to foster gold debts abroad and prostration of the industries at home, because this double fostering tends to increase our debts, public and private, and especially as we are going to base our currency all on specie, we must have these foreign debts to take the specie away from us in the shape of interest, then we will be without specie, without money basis, without money of course, and without price for anything; then will we be in good condition for our merciful British nobility benefactors, and their generous coadjutors on these shores, to take us, with this little heritage of ours, into their kind care and keeping, both for ownership and government, civil and military. Then we shall have nothing to do but to hew their wood, draw their water, cultivate their soil, and fight such battles as they see fit, for their own glory and amusement, to set in array for us.

The demonetizing of silver, as was done by act of Congress of February 12, 1873, is a part of this same scheme, taken in connection with issuing of foreign gold bonds, to get the country destitute of specie, and in that condition force specie payments, and thereby create a sweeping transfer of the people's property to a moneyed few, in the same manner as was done in England, and to establish the same condition of things here as there, to wit: a noble few to own the country and rule it, and a vassalage to perform the work. If this is the destiny intended for us by the founders of our Government, I have labored under a great mistake all my life.

MARVIN WARREN.

NOTE.—In place of over-producing, we have imported, in the last ten years, over one thousand million dollars ($1,000,000,000) in excess of what we were able to pay by sales of exports, proving positively that over-importation is one cause of our financial troubles, and under-production to be the real cause, instead of over-industry. These "balances" must have been paid by *sending our bonds abroad*, thus alienating our national debt, and having to pay the interest abroad.

To reduce our imports two hundred millions annually is giving our laboring and producing classes annually two hundred million dollars of additional employments. This can easily be done by means of proper tariff law, without cost, and without borrowing.

A large increase of duties on foreign industries of our own kind, is no increase of taxes upon our own people, but the reverse, being an increase of wealth to them, as our Government requires only a certain amount of revenue for its support, which is as large under low as under protective duties. The difference and gain to our people is the increase of employment and gold, corresponding with the reduction made in the amount and gold cost of our imports.

The unparalleled prosperity of France, fresh from her disastrous war, can only be attributed to her wise protective policy, which results in having annually a balance of trade of over one hundred millions in her favor.

I favor a free list and low duties for all necessary productions imported, which we ourselves do not produce and sell.

A tariff for revenue, and not for the protection of American industries, would quickly cause our great republic to be reduced to the level of European countries—for workingmen, a country to migrate from to seek elsewhere work and a living.

There are two ways to renew specie payments. One is by contracting and destroying our present and only money and continue low duties, and leave all in poverty, so that eventually we cannot import for the want of funds, which would necessarily largely reduce imports and give us the balance of trade. The other way is a large increase of duties, which would cause a like large reduction of imports, and cause a large demand for American employments and productions at home, to supply the reduction made in imports.

Our Congress should make our paper currency as good as gold, a legal tender for import duties, and at the same time largely increase the duties, to cover the loss in the difference of value in gold and currency, and to largely reduce imports below trade exports.

Whenever our nation's annual exports (exclusive of gold debt payments sent abroad) will not fully meet and pay all foreign demands, both for purchased imports, debt, and interest annually due abroad, then we should increase duties to retrench and economize our nation's foreign extravagance in purchasing imports. Then our country could not be impoverished as now, either of its own employments or its own gold.

When either of the real producers of our country's wealth, manufacturers, miners, or farmers, are impoverished by foreign competition, then all are made to suffer, because each one's productions add to the one total production of our country.

There is only one quick way to possess an abundance of specie, and that is this way, which is a very old one—Do not spend so much specie with other nations for foreign productions. Manufacture and produce more for ourselves. This will give our people more specie and more employment and wealth. A high tariff alone will do this.

The protectionists of foreign industries in Congress are easily known. They are always in favor of taxing heavily American productions three hundred per cent., and would tax tea and coffee, which our poor people must have and should not be taxed, because it will not increase our employments, as duties on foreign industries would do.

Our American people cannot support all other nations' industries and our own beside, as low duties now cause us to do. A tariff law for American industries alone would dissolve this ruinous and unnatural division of our market, as was found necessary to do after the bankruptcies of 1837 and 1857, to our country's immediate relief from depression of business.

GEORGE W. DEAN.

FREE TRADE—ITS EFFECTS ON THE FARMER.

IN my letter to the Hon. James Brooks in reply to a speech made by him in favor of free trade, I made the following offer, saying that

"I am informed from Washington that Mr. Brooks is now ready 'to mount on a peddler's wagon and ride through the agricultural districts of the country exhibiting hoes, shovels, axes, bars, chains, rods, knives, forks, cottons and woollens, to demonstrate to the eyes of the people the enormous taxation imposed on them by the existing tariffs.'

"Before he commences this journey among the farmers, I propose to share with him a large part of the expense, on condition that he will inform the farmers as he goes through the country that, according to Mr. Wells's report, there are one million of men now employed in the manufacture of those articles so indispensable to every farmer.

"I want him to ascertain from the farmers how many millions of bushels of their grain and all other agricultural products are annually consumed by these hundreds of thousands of the workingmen of our country. I want him to be very particular, as he goes along, to show the farmers how perfectly insignificant the amount of grain is that has been sold abroad, when compared with the amount that is annually consumed by the men now employed in making the various articles he enumerates. It will be well, as he comes in contact with the farmers, to ascertain where they expect to find a market when those hundreds of thousands that now consume their produce are forced to turn farmers and come in competition with them for a market.

"I hope Mr. Brooks will quote from Mr. Wells's report, where he states ' that the American agriculturist does not command his own price in a foreign market, but the price commands him,' as he is compelled ' to sell at the price offered in London, the central market of the world,' where farm labor is hired for one-half the price paid for it in this country.

"It will be a matter of the greatest interest for the farmers to know that Mr. Wells says ' there are now one million of skilled artisans in our country, making the largest and most valuable consuming class in this community.'

"Mr. Brooks should tell the farmers that these are the men, with their families, employers and laborers, that consume a large part of all they have to sell, and are now paying them more than they could get in any other part of the world.

"I hope Mr. Brooks will be sure, as he passes through the country, to tell the farmers that he and his friends are doing all they can to withdraw the legal-tender notes, and bring about a speedy return to specie payments, and that, notwithstanding, we are a debtor country to an amount nearly equal to our national debt.

"He can assure the farmers that, as soon as our bank paper is payable in specie on demand, there will be some four or five dollars of paper afloat for every silver or gold dollar in the country.

"He should assure the farmers that when all our paper money is made payable in specie on demand, it will prove the most certain means that can be used to ' fertilize the rich man's field by the sweat of the poor man's brow.'

"It will do this by ensuring the periodical return of those scenes of panic, pressure and general bankruptcy and ruin that have so often changed the values of all property and labor some twenty-five or fifty per cent. in a single year, whenever it was for the interest of foreign creditors or merchants at home to withdraw a few extra millions from our banks, as they did in '57, when a withdrawal of only seven millions produced the panic of that year, which sunk the values of all the property of our country to the amount of thousands of millions of dollars. These millions were taken from the farmers, mechanics and merchants who were in debt, and put in the possession of those who had the means to buy at the ruinous rates at which property of all kinds was compelled to be sold, thus making, as it ever must, the rich richer, and the poor poorer.

"Mr. Brooks should sound an alarm as he goes through the country, and say to all that there can be no security for any man that is in debt until our general government shall perform its most important duty, which is not only to establish a just system of money, weights and measures, but a system of legal-tender paper money, in amount equal to the amount put in circulation at the end of the war by the necessities of the government.

"Such a legal-tender paper money would be a bond and mortgage on the whole property of the country and a bond of union among the states, and would leave gold and silver to be an article of commerce in the hands of those who hold it.

"Mr. Brooks will perform a most valuable service to the country if he will tell the farmers that Dr. Franklin says that the American people under the old colonial government were so immoderately fond of the manufactures and superfluities of foreign countries 'that they could not be restrained from purchasing them,' 'because such laws, if made, would be immediately repealed as prejudicial to the trade and interest of Great Britain.' Dr. Franklin then adds that 'it seems hard, therefore, to draw all their real money from them, and then refuse them the privilege of using paper instead of it.'

"Mr. Brooks will perform a most valuable service to the country by showing the farmers that the absenteeism that has ruined Ireland was nothing more the turning of a hundred small farms into one large grazing farm, that can be managed by a single individual, instead of making a home for the hundred individual farmers.

"He should show the farmers that Ireland has been impoverished by the same policy that England tried to force on her American colonies, as will appear by the following facts of British legislation :

"In 1710 a law was enacted in the House of Commons that declared the erecting of manufactories in the colonies tended to lessen their dependence on Great Britain.

"In 1732 the exportation of hats from province to province, and the number of apprentices, was limited.

"In 1750 the erection of any mill or engine for slitting or rolling iron was prohibited.

"In 1765 the exportation of artisans was prohibited under a heavy penalty.

"In 1781 utensils required for the manufacture of wool or silk were prohibited.

"In 1782 the prohibition was extended to artificers in printing calicos, muslins, or linens.

"In 1785 the prohibition was extended to tools used in iron or steel manufacture, and to workmen employed.

"In 1799 it was so extended as to even embrace colliers."

All classes should gather wisdom by reflecting on the history and the experience of the past.

Free trade is beautiful in theory, and will be in practice where all things are equal and peaceful in the relations of nations, and rapid transit shall go far to annihilate space.

Our government having allowed and used paper money until the day's labor has been made to cost at least one-third more than a similar day's labor would cost in other countries, to bring about an equality in trade will require a tariff based on the difference in the cost that will purchase a day's labor in our country as compared with that of foreign countries.

If the farmers desire to secure for themselves a reliable market and the highest price for their product, they must use the means best calculated to effect that object—they must encourage the manufacture of the articles they consume and have them made as near their homes as possible. This should be done wherever good raw materials can be found that can be put into forms of usefulness with as small expense of labor in this country as in any part of the world.

If I am not mistaken our country will rise out of its great embarrassment in a way that would astonish the world, if our government would perform what was and is its first and most important duty.

The Constitution made it the duty of Congress to adopt measures that will "establish justice;" that is the only means by which the "common welfare can be promoted."

To establish justic for a nation there must be created and maintained a just and uniform system of money, weights and measures.

It is of the greatest importance that all the paper money allowed by the government should be made as unyielding in its power to pay debts as the yard-stick or the pound weight.

Our government having been literally compelled to issue and use a legal-tender paper money in order to save the nation's life, has, by its use, caused the whole property of the country to be measured by its purchasing power. By this use of paper money the government has created a most solemn obligation on its part to do no act to increase or diminish the amount of paper money beyond the absolute necessities of the government. As an increase of the amount would inflate prices without increasing real values, in the same proportion a diminution of currency must cause all property to shrink in price, and thereby put it out of the power of the people to pay the national debt.

One thing is certain that the national debts can never be paid by a governmental policy that shrinks the currency, destroys values, paralyzes industry, enforces idleness, and brings wretchedness and ruin to the homes of millions of the American people. It is equally true that Americans can never buy anything cheap from foreign countries that must be bought at the expense of leaving our own good raw materials unused, and our own labor unemployed. It should be remembered that neither gold, silver, copper, nickel nor paper are money without the stamp of the government upon it. The Constitution has made it the duty of Congress to coin the money of our country and regulate the value thereof, and fix a standard of weights and measures, as the only possible means by which commerce can be regulated between foreign nations and among the several States.

PETER COOPER.

THE
UNMEASURED IMPORTANCE
OF AN
UNFLUCTUATING NATIONAL CURRENCY
OVER WHICH THE GOVERNMENT HAS ENTIRE CONTROL.

AN INTERVIEW OF A REPORTER WITH PETER COOPER, AS PUBLISHED IN *The New York Herald.*

REPORTER.—Mr. Cooper, what do you think of the late letter of Mr. Reverdy Johnson on the subject of the currency?

MR. COOPER.—I think that Mr. Johnson has there given some very wholesome truths, and for a man of his intelligence, he has made some remarkable mistakes. He says truly that "the question of currency is now the most important one before the country. It rises, or should rise, far above mere party contests."

He adds, with great propriety, that "the subject of currency affects the permanent welfare of every citizen—the prosperity of the country, and the reputation of the Government."

He then adds that "it must be obvious to every reflecting mind that a currency ought to be as far removed from fluctuations of value as possible."

I believe that Mr. Johnson is unquestionably right in saying that, "with a currency, subject at times to a depreciation and at times to appreciation, the consequences can but be injurious; and the extent of injury will be in proportion to the changes of value."

Mr. Johnson then states, what I believe to be an entire mistake, that "the experience of the world has long since demonstrated that gold and silver alone constitute a safe currency."

As to what control the Government has over money, this will find its best answer in the language of the Constitution, where it says that "CONGRESS SHALL HAVE POWER TO LAY AND COLLECT TAXES,"—"to borrow money, to regulate commerce,"—"to coin money and regulate the value thereof," a most important function, and "to make all laws which are necessary and proper for carrying into execution the foregoing powers, and all other powers vested by the Constitution in the Government of the United States." These are necessary to "establish justice and promote the welfare of the nation."

REP.—But what are your views, Mr. Cooper, on this question of currency in relation to the Government at the present time?

MR. C.—I think the currency question has been managed by the Government very much in the interests of the moneyed classes, and very poorly in the interests of the people. Let us look at some of the facts.

In the year 1860, a civil war broke out in this country which threatened the integrity and life of this nation. At this time, the expenses of the Government increased very largely over its current expenses in time of peace.

In fact, it became necessary for the Government to borrow money and place a large debt on the shoulders of posterity, in order to transmit unimpaired the priceless boon of free institutions, and a powerful and self-protecting Republic of States. Now, a nation is not like a private individual, who, if he wants money, must go and borrow it of some one else because he has no resource of his own from which money can come, but only some security which he may give that the money will be returned. A nation has, always, indefinite resources on which to draw, and yet can give no LEGAL security for the payment of its obligations. Money itself is a creature of law, and the sovereign prerogative of the State. The Government can make anything a legal tender, and it is only a question of expediency what it shall make. But it can give no legal security for payment of its debts, because a sovereign State cannot be sued, nor can you replevin on its property, except by war. To be sure, a nation may borrow as a private individual from another, or from a corporation ; but in doing so, it puts itself in a false position, and makes itself subject to the lender, as in any other debtor, to the extent of his debt—except that the creditor has no other resource for collection BUT TO TAKE ENTIRE CONTROL OF THAT GOVERNMENT, as respects its financial policy. Therefore, the people and their interests may be shoved aside, for they become antagonistic to the class who are the creditors, who naturally desire to make their loans at the least cost and the highest interest. But if the people themselves in their solid interests and unity, as represented by a Republican Government, were both the debtors and creditors of all the public debt, then there would be no antagonism between the debtors and creditors.

REP.—But do you mean to say, Mr. Cooper, that a Government has no need, and should never borrow from individuals and corporations ?

MR. C.—I think that a republic like ours, with its forty millions, with its enormous extent of unoccupied land, its wonderful resources, and its enterprising people—equally marvellous for their growth and the increase of their wealth within the century—has no need to borrow from anybody. Why should this people borrow, as a private debtor? If, in their sovereign capacity through the Government and under constitutional and legal forms, they can lay under contribution the whole property, and the services of every man, in protecting the lives and property of all, they certainly can issue tokens of this undoubted fact, in the shape of legal tenders ; and these become, by this act of sovereignty, the money of the country, the measure and the means of exchanges. The people who give them, in their sovereign capacity, must take them in their private capacity, and again receive them in their sovereign capacity as the Government, for taxes. This makes their circulation and their use. But the significance of these paper " legal tenders " is that they are tokens of such service or material rendered to the Government ; and they are also promises to render an equal amount of money, service, or useful material in exchange, to the holder, by the Government.

The paid functions of Government, or the equivalent taxes, form a just and adequate basis for the redemption of a paper currency, and furnish a better legal tender than gold or silver, for the domestic purposes of trade, if properly regulated by the Government; hence, I would *demonetize* gold and silver, except as mere tokens of value, and make Government paper, *exclusively*, the *legal tender*.

This is a very important proposition, in the discussion of national finances, and demands a clear explanation.

1st. If a private note of hand or a bank-note is "good" in proportion to the known credit and resources of the individual or the bank, so is that of the Government, and in a superior degree, as the Government has a larger credit and more resources than an individual or a bank.

2d. An individual or a bank pays its debts by means of its credits, or the valid claims either may have on others; so does the Government; and the valid claims of Government are all represented in rightful taxes, imposed for its proper functions and employments.

Government, on one side, is the giver of sound credit, represented by its paper; the validity and redeeming basis of this paper is in the fact, that the community is indebted to the Government in the shape of taxes for so much service and material as may be necessary to carry on its proper function, and pay its officers for services rendered to the public; this creates an obligation on the part of the public to receive Government paper for "value received." Thus the circulation is complete. As the creditors of an individual or of a bank receive its paper, and pass it to debtors, who in their turn pay their debts to the bank with its own paper, so the Government puts out its paper for service and labor, and redeems its notes by the taxes due. This is the sort of legal tender and currency we need, as undoubted representative for value received, as gold or silver. Regulated in volume by the amount of taxation which the people are willing to bear in order to support Government; for not a dollar of it can be issued except for "value received," and under the watchful guard of the whole machinery of Government. Where, then, is the danger of inflation, except in time of war, or by a temporary wresting of the Government from the hands of the people? One of these contingencies is comparatively rare, and not without its compensations, in the objects attained by the war. The other is a very remote and improbable contingency, in a country like this—hardly worth taking into account, in this argument.

On the other hand, bank-paper is sure to be inflated sooner or later, without compensation, but with general loss or disaster. For, if it is to be redeemed by specie, the paper cannot be kept within the limits of redemption and satisfy at the same time the demand for credit. If a part of it becomes irredeemable, the whole of it becomes irredeemable at a blow.

But if the paper merely represents credit, it is the real capital and claims or assets of the bank that must support that credit; and the history of banking clearly shows that the inevitable tendency is, that bank circulation gets in advance of its real capital or assets; because the assets are sure to fall greatly in the market if they are brought quickly forward to pay its debts, as is the case in times of panic. The sudden curtailment of its loans from time to time can alone keep up a system of banks, and this is sure to bring on ruin and panic in business. Not so with a Government currency, regulated solely by Government taxes and dues. It must be comparatively steady and unfluctuating as the taxes; and hence, the general credits based on such a currency cannot fluctuate enough to produce great inflations, in times of peace, and the consequent reactions and panics in business.

REP. Why not? It seems to me that Government paper may be subject to great inflations, as well as bank paper, and the expanded credits that arise from such inflations must suffer contraction, sooner or later, by a natural law; for the "pay day" must come at last, and few who are eager to borrow can meet the payment. Government paper may be inflated on a more gigantic scale than bank paper, as our last war proved.

MR. C. That was a war measure, and was justified for the same reason as the war. But the mischief did not arise from the expansion of the currency, which sent a vivifying influence throughout all our industries, and produced the most prosperous times this country ever had; but it was the contraction of the currency which brought the distress; and this was neither necessary nor called for by any advantage accruing.

The eagerness with which our currency was funded by foreign bond-holders was owing to the fact that our government gave such high rates of interest, as compared with other governments, and promised both principal and interest in gold when the paper that bought the bonds was at forty or sixty per cent. discount on the gold. Was that patriotic or necessary? To pay so much of the debt of the nation before it was due, as Mr. McCullough boasted was his object, and to turn so large a part of the currency which fed the industry of the people, into bonds that taxed that industry, was a very short-sighted policy for the Government to pursue.

REP. But how is the Government always to keep its paper issues, in time of peace, on a par with the standard adopted as a unit of value— *so much weight of silver or gold, in the coin dollar?* This standard gives meaning to the stamp on the paper, as equivalent to, or exchangeable for, so much value, as the number of dollars stamped on the paper, measured by the *standard coin dollar.* This is a necessary starting-point in measuring values, as a certain length or a certain weight is to the yard-stick, or to the pound weight.

MR. C. That is very true. It is necessary to have some substantial and recognized standard of value to start with, in money, whether it be coin or currency. This standard, however, might be a pound of cotton of a certain fineness, or a pound of tobacco of a certain quality, as far as giving a standard value to the paper was concerned. It is also true that the paper must have *some* exchangable value as money, as measured by a standard; and the Government cannot give it that exchangeable value, in *any* quantity, by merely stamping the paper as worth so much. What we want is a *paper money*, made equal in exchangeable value to gold or silver of a certain standard.

Now the Government keeps its promise to pay in three ways. First, by accepting these paper promises, as they may be called, for all taxes and dues to the Government. Secondly, by compelling every individual to accept them in payment of all debts. And finally, by redeeming them in that which the holder of the currency shall accept as equivalent value, the Government Bonds, thus distributing burdens and benefits over the whole country.

REP.—But this is only compelling individuals to accept one token of debt for another. How is the public debt to be paid at last, and how shall we get out of this vortex of promises to pay?

MR. C.—In one sense, there is no need to get out of this vortex; the planets move in a vortex; the whole of society, and the universe, as far as we see it, move in vortices. This is the grand law of motion and circulation. But circulation also signifies growth, and ministers to it. Parts of every circulating medium settle down to something solid, which makes a part of the organism, and keeps up its integrity, and adds to its growth. The circulating medium of money settles down, at last, into something solid in interest and property, under the same law of conversion that makes each drop of blood contribute to bone, muscle, or other organ of the body. For instance, New York City is building a great series of piers and wharves, for the accommodation of its present and future commerce and trade. It is demonstrable that these piers and wharves will pay in rents to the city, not only the interest but the principal of all the money invested, in twenty years. The city issues its bonds for this work, which represent a certain amount of interest and principal. But the city, not having the right to issue money, offers its bonds for sale to the banks, or to private individuals, which are henceforth alienated from the possession of the city, in order to get the money or currency to pay for labor and material in this public work. You might ask, why should not the city keep these bonds in its own safes, and issue the money for current expenses on its own authority and credit? I answer: Because that would be an act of too great a local sovereignty—though it is no more than is now virtually conceded to local banks. Let the general Government, then, in its sovereignty, make such a currency, so based and secured, a legal tender. Then, when this work is done, and begins to pay to the city rents, let the income be applied to the extinguishment of the bonds, as well as keeping it in repair. This is what I mean by settling down a circulating medium or currency INTO SOLID MATERIAL, and capital, organized into permanent use.

This makes a circulating medium always expanding and always contracting into a solid form. The true design and highest function of currency and credit are to encourage and stimulate industry and enterprise in useful forms, and to promote the work by giving the very tools with which it can be done. It represents the material value of the products of labor in process, and not yet complete; for which it provides merely the current wages or support, till the fruit of labor comes to maturity, when that pays for all.

REP.—Mr. Cooper, what is your opinion of the present banking system?

MR. C.—Financial institutions are very useful, and will always be necessary to carry on the commerce, trade, and industries of the country. They concentrate capital in financial centres, from which it is again distributed all over the country where it is most wanted. I regard a banking system, properly confined to the collecting and loaning out of the real capital, in aid of all useful enterprises, as a national blessing. But, incidentally, banks do a great deal of mischief by doing business, in part, on a bad system and on false assumptions. They often confound the distinction between credit and capital, and do business on credit without capital. Credit must be distinguished from capital. Credit cannot be borrowed or lent; it can only be *given*, or exercised by one mind toward another. Capital is borrowed and lent, for it can be passed from hand to hand. The one is very necessary to the other; for capital supports credit, and credit sets capital to work in multiplying capital; thus preventing the latter from waste and loss of it. Credit and capital, therefore, naturally imply each other, and are necessary to a mutual existence. It is death or disaster to both to separate them. Financial troubles may come from the want of capital, or credit, or both.

REP.—But how do you account for our present financial troubles?

MR. C.—Our present financial troubles doubtless began in the want of sufficient capital, at command, to carry on certain great and small enterprises to successful issues, in which the parties asked more credit than there was capital to back it. But when these parties failed, it gave a shock to credit; this paralyzed the active use of capital, and withdrew it still more from the support of credit, until a "panic" came. For people did not know where or when this trouble would stop. Like a crowd in a public building, the rush for escape, when there is an alarm given, bears no proportion to the danger; but it soon substitutes a far worse source of destruction and suffering in the "panic." And, as in this case, the trouble is soon relieved by opening wide the doors of egress, so, in financial panics and troubles, the true remedy is *expansion* of credits and capital, and not *contraction*.

REP.—But what have the banks to do with all this?

MR. C.—I have not, as yet, mentioned the chief source of our financial troubles and panics; it is the false system which our financial institutions mix up with what is true in them. They rest much business on a "false bottom," which may drop out at any time. They lend their credit without sufficient capital to back it, and call it "lending capital." The old system of banks which some are now anxious to renew, lent out three and five dollars in paper to one of gold kept for redemption. Their capital was to the credit they assumed as one to three, five, or more; consequently, when the capital promised by the paper was called for, as sooner or later it must be, so much of the credit came to naught, involving loss to the banks, not of their *capital*, but of their *sham credits*. But these "sham credits" meanwhile had transferred a great deal of real property from the hands to which the property belonged to those who held the temporary credit. This injustice and wrong comes to the surface, at short intervals, in the shape of "panics" and financial distress. The present system of banks, although not doing business on a specie basis, yet introduces a "false bottom" to business in another way; they do a large amount of business on their depositors' capital. If the "deposits" are called for faster than the bank can return them, the bank fails in its credit, but loses comparatively little. The loss of **real** capital falls chiefly on the trusting "depositors." This system goes smoothly, transferring property and facilitating trade, till the capital implied by the credit is needed in substantial form. The promise can no longer be put off; the payment is required; then the false props are all taken away, and financial ruin is the result; credit given to brains, muscle, industry, and enterprise is one thing, and credit given to actual products and estates is another; but still, credit based on either is a *real credit*, because brain-work and enterprise are just as real as the material products to which they give existence. But credit based on mere *assumption* or *supposition* of capital, is not properly based. It is a bogus credit, that looks like the real thing, but sooner or later fails entirely.

If the Government does not require the banks to redeem their notes either in gold or in bonds, or if it allows them to coin their deposits into loans, it gives them the privilege of giving others the use simply of the banks' credit, far beyond their capital. The banks have done too much of that business already.

REP.—What, then, would be your remedy for this false system of banking?

MR. C.—The true remedy for all these financial shams and pretences that transfer the property of the real owners to those who are mere financial agents, is to permit the banks to do business only on real money or legal tender, interconvertible with bonds. This will convert all money into a safety fund, and make it unnecessary for banks to loan their deposits, which they can always fund in government securities, and have them again "on call." But this system will expand the real credits which the banks can give, based all on real capital, and make such credits equal to the wants of a new and expanding country like ours, with institutions that stimulate the industries, the enterprises, and the powers of this people, beyond anything that history can yet show of any people.

Some people mistake altogether, or put a false construction on transactions called credit, which are not so, strictly. For instance, if you go to a bank or a broker, and give your bonds, stocks, or securities in mortgages, or any other shape, and borrow a certain amount on the same, that is not strictly giving and receiving credit; it is simply a sale of property, WITH AN IF. For if you fail to pay on a certain day, there will be transference of property, but no credit lost. In fact, the man borrows the use of credit in the shape of money, but makes it good on his own property. Therefore, the borrower himself gives the only foundation there is to that credit. But if the man is about to improve a farm, or build a factory, and borrows money to buy material or employ labor, which money can only be returned if he succeeds in his enterprise, and produces a piece of property on the strength of that credit, which may return all that has been invested in it, THAT IS REAL CREDIT. That money represents the credit or faith given to an enterprise and a work in progress, which may result in some valuable property; but if it does not, the credit is lost, and both borrower and creditor are sufferers by the failure. There is certainly a difference between borrowing money on the security of a tangible property, equivalent to the sum borrowed, and borrowing money on the faith of the powers, intelligence, and capacity for work which will create a piece of property if given the credit and opportunity which the money furnishes. This last is the only credit that the poor need, or can ask. But it is essential in the world, and there ought to be no limit to such credit, except what is sufficient to set every man and woman to some useful work.

This makes credit in finance, like faith in religion, " the evidence of things unseen and the substance of things hoped for." This process is going on every day, for there can be no growth or development in society without it. But now governments, general and local, mix up their own credit, or seek altogether to sustain the public, on private credit. The sovereign authority of making this circulating medium of money, which ought to be backed by the highest, the most permanent and reliable ability to pay, is thought safer by many when the weight of responsibility is put upon private shoulders or those of corporations, than when it is resting upon the broad and secure basis of a nation organized under republican institutions, " by the people and for the people," and pledging its wealth and honor as a nation for the redemption of all debts incurred for the public weal.

This enslaves a people, through the very machinery of free institutions and republican forms, to the will, the caprice, or the greed of particular classes of individuals that control money. The Government should never be a borrower, except of such labor and material as is necessary to public service. This it must acknowledge by tokens of its own creation and stamp, and pay at maturity, by means of taxes on property which this very credit has brought into existence, and, as it were, SOLIDIFIED into a permanent source of income, such as a great public work, or any form of fixed capital, or, still more a nation's life and prosperity. What I said New York was doing, and might do with regard to her public works, could be done by the Government on a far grander scale.

REP. But, Mr. Cooper, I do not understand what you call " *real money*." Is not gold and silver the only real money, and all other forms merely representative of value ?

MR. C. No, sir ; gold and silver is not the only real money. The precious metals are constituted money by the same authority, and for the same purpose, that paper may be employed as money. Money is purely a creature of law. All metals must be coined by authority before they can pass as money; and the proof of this is in the fact that the precious metal stamped and made into money by one Government will not pass as such under the jurisdiction of another. Foreign coin is never a " *legal tender*." This being the case, we must look to something else as the *essential characteristic* of money than the exchangeable value of the substance of which it is made, which makes it a commodity in any market. The value of money depends upon two conditions only, both of which are governed by law, and only one of which depends upon demand and supply, as do the values of pure commodities. The first condition of giving value to money is to make it a legal tender for all private debts, and also the taxes and dues of Government. This gives it a purely legal value, and makes it like a mortgage on property, and also like a note of hand, issued by the Government, and secured as well as redeemed by its taxing power and authority over the whole property of the country. The second condition of value in money is that it should be *rentable*, like any other capital, or bear some interest, to the lender. This can also be fixed by law, as in laws of usury. But the Government can go further than this in giving a legal value to its own legal tender in the shape of paper money; it can make this legal tender fundable at a fixed rate of interest, payable either in coin or in its equivalent paper. The bonds of the Government thus give a secondary or vendible value to the paper money, which makes it like any other commodity, rentable, and of a market value. This being a fact, it shows that in all the proper qualities of *real money* paper money can be made such by the Government that issues it, as gold or silver coin—it will pay all your debts and taxes, and also has a market value, because it is rentable or loanable.

REP. But not abroad; you cannot send this money abroad.

MR. C. No, you cannot send any money abroad except as commodity, vendible, which takes from it the character of money. But this is an advantage in the use of paper money, which, being an indispensable measure of values at home, and a necessary means of exchange, should never be taken from the trade and domestic uses of one country to be exported as commodity to another.

REP. How, then, shall we keep up its value on a par with that of other countries, so that we shall not be buying abroad with one standard of value and selling at home with another?

MR. C. That is no great hardship, compared to being left without sufficient money to do business and pay the wages of labor. But the true remedy for this is to encourage industry in every way at home, so as to have a surplus of production in things that can find a market abroad, and thus keep *even the "balance of trade,"* which keeps the money of different countries at a par value. For this purpose nothing is more conducive than a good, sound currency at home, in sufficient quantities, at all times, to keep up all the exchanges and the payment of wages needed for our own domestic industries, and to protect our own people from too great a competition with the cheap labor of Europe by a proper *revenue tariff*. This is the commercial and financial sheet-anchor of any people. A tariff taxes the surplus of other countries which finds its way to our own markets for the support of the Government that protects, and in a manner furnishes that market. It taxes chiefly the capital of the foreign manufacturer and the domestic importer of this surplus production, because they must find a market *somewhere*, and therefore sell at whatever rates they can get in competition with the industry at home, helped by the tariff; and it taxes the consumer, who will buy luxuries, that leave our own good raw material unused and our own domestic labor unemployed—for I assume that nothing but what interferes with these shall be subject to tariff.

REP. But gold and silver have an intrinsic and *inalienable* market value all over the world; whereas your Government paper money—currency or bonds—has purely a legal value, and may be real to-day but nothing to-morrow, depending entirely upon the stability of Government

Mr. C. So has all paper representing true value and made the medium of exchange—a "note of hand," a mortgage, or a bank-note—they all derive their virtual value from the law that constitutes them repre sentatives of value. Yet modern commerce and trade cannot dispense with these and reduce all their transactions to barter, or to paying bal lances with gold and silver. They assume the stability of governments, without which neither property nor life are secure. What security would gold give if there were no Government to protect it? All these paper obligations, used as medium of exchange, and having a market value, are based upon the faith, the property, and stability of individuals or corporations, with the further sanction of law. We desire, as a medium of exchange, a legal tender that shall represent the whole taxable prop erty of the country and the stability and faith of the Government. It seems to me that if a corporation can issue valuable paper, much more can a Government, backed by the resources of a whole people, do the same.

Rep. But how has the Government failed in its duty to the people?

Mr. C. The Government, during the progress of this war of the rebel lion, felt obliged to employ more service and material in the struggle for existence with a powerful foe than it could pay from any immediate re sources. It felt obliged to borrow this material and service on credit. It issued its bonds; but the Government went begging, as New York does, to private individuals and to corporations to furnish another credit, called money, for the purpose of paying current expenses The limited amount of this latter credit which was at the service of the Government made the bonds sell at great discount on their face.

Gold was sought for, when there was not enough of this product of labor within reach to represent a tithe of the credit sought by the Gov ernment. Now, if the Government could issue one form of credit, why go begging for another?

This occurred at last to some of those in authority and paper money tokens were issued. Under a patriotic impulse and faith in this nation and its resources, some of these were made receivable for all dues of the Government, and others made convertible into 5-20 bonds at par— at the will of the holder. This made and kept the currency nearly at par with gold, even in the DARK days of CIVIL WAR. This will always keep the national currency equal in value to gold, provided it is the only paper in circulation, and the exclusive legal tender, and fully re deemed by taxes, duties and Government bonds, at the option of the holder. The Government thus has a three-fold method of redeeming its paper, whereas the banks have but one method, and that is by specie. This method must fail them, at times, because the specie will go out of the country, when the balances of trade are against us, in quantities sufficient to interfere with redemption. "Bank paper," as Calhoun says, "is cheap to those who make it, but dear, very dear to those who use it." Banks can never redeem their paper in specie, except in times of expanding credits, when very little specie is wanted. During such times the banks secure them selves on real property, but the public is secured on the bank paper only in its promise to pay coin. But this national currency was found to be far safer than any private or corporation tokens of in debtedness, and threatened to supersede all other tokens of indebtedness as a currency. Thus the great power and moneyed advantage which the making of such tokens, and the passing of them into circulation, gave to private corporations would be destroyed. Those who had personal interests involved took the alarm; they regarded their "vested rights" infringed upon, and they had influence enough with the then existing administration and Congress to have that law repealed. They represented that gold would be drained from the country, and our purchasing power abroad reduced to nothing.

"How should we get our silks, our wines, and our cigars?" The importers, brokers, and money changers of all kinds, as well as the speculators in gold, would find their occupation gone! It was in vain to tell these alarmists that gold was one of the many products of industry, and those who needed it must buy it at the market price, which no legislation could control, though it might falsify and interfere with the natural price of gold for a time. That it was of small importance to the people at large, how much gold, measured as a commodity, a legal tender would buy, but of much greater importance how much bread could be got for the same money. If paper is made a legal tender, under the same advantages as gold, that is, that it should always represent a real and exchangeable value in interest-bearing property, and receivable for all debts, public and private, the paper would then be on a par with gold as money. No! these parties understood, as they thought, THEIR OWN INTERESTS, and under specious but false pretences and arguments induced Congress to repeal the law that made the currency of the United States receivable for all dues to the Government, and also the law making legal tender notes fundible into Government securities at par. The repeal of the law permitting holders of legal tenders to convert them at their option into interest-bearing bonds was the most cruel act of injustice that was ever inflicted on the American people. From thence have come most of the financial troubles and disasters of which so much complaint is made at the present time. Our bonds were rushed abroad, to be exchanged for luxuries and for gold at sixty cents on the dollar, instead of being taken by our own people at par.

Millions of gold go abroad to pay interest to foreign bondholders, instead of being paid to our own people.

A policy of rapid contraction was then inspired into the Government; when, the necessities of the war being over, further issues of bonds were made and currency was withdrawn, and all credits began to contract, as a natural and inevitable consequence. This brought on one of those irrational conditions in human affairs which we call a "panic," that brought down credit at once to the zero point, and shrunk the value of all property.

REP.—But, Mr. Cooper, do you not think that personal extravagance, rash speculations, and over-production generally, have much to do with the present financial embarrassments?

MR. C.—In a restricted sense all these causes lie at the basis of much financial embarrassment: But all of them put together will not account for the fact that there are over two mi.lions of workmen, operatives, and employees, out of work at this time in this country, or on short allowance of work, who three years ago had ample employment. Speculations ruin a few in financial centres and cause merely a change of ownership in property, and the loss of credit to those engaged in such speculations. Personal extravagance is chiefly confined to a few rich men, for most people care not or are unable to indulge beyond their means.

Over-production and undue importations seem to be the most plausible of the reasons offered for the present financial embarrassments; because, when goods accumulate in merchants' hands, and products multiply in the factories, the mines, and farms, without a corresponding demand and consumption, the most obvious cause or explanation is, that there have been too much production and importation. But have these been too much for the demand and consumption previously existing, or subsequently? The true law of supply, and the stimulus, and the reason for production, is demand; this comes first, and the former comes last in the order of nature. There might be a production that overtakes and passes an existing consumption in particular cases; but it is well also to examine, in a general way, whether any cause has paralyzed consumption. Now, it has been seen that the systematic and constant contraction of Government credits naturally induced the contraction of all other credits; this finally brought on a panic that acted like a paralysis on all credit; this led inevitably to the stoppage of so much active industry and work as to take away the PURCHASING power of a great many, and to stop a large part of the previously existing consumption and demand. Hence, the over-production (so-called) has been merely an accumulation of products, due to UNDER-CONSUMPTION. The proof of this lies in the fact, as I have said, of so many industrious people being thrown out of work, and in the statistics of the country, with regard to its exportations and importations the last few years. In this connection the opinion of President Grant, as expressed in his annual message of 1873, is important.

REP.—But how would you have prevented this sad condition of things from coming on? It appears to me it arose naturally out of the irredeemable nature of the currency. Gold and silver have always been regarded as the currency and money of the world. A man that is in debt naturally desires to get out of it as soon as he can. Why, then, should not a nation exercise economy or "contraction" for the same end?

MR. C.—Because "contraction" in finance is not the same thing as economy in private life. "Contraction" in the finances of a country means the stoppage of a certain amount of the industry and exchanges going on in the nation, by reason of the contraction of the credit by which these are sustained. It means factories stopped, and men thrown out of work, and distress of families for want of the means to buy bread. Now, THIS IS ALL WRONG, and it arises out of a false financial system, not adapted to the wants of a people whose wants and powers are all the time expanding, by reason of a natural increase in the population, and by our possession of a new country of unlimited natural resources, which yet need to be developed by the EXPANSION and not the contraction of the credit which capital gives to labor.

But, I grant you, there is a contraction on the side of debt in the finances of a country which is always desirable. It is in that SOLIDIFYING process which I have already described, that turns currency into fixed capital, as the blood is deposited into bones, flesh, and organism. The bond, and the currency based on it, must be paid and destroyed as evidence of that debt, as soon as value received for them can be turned into some permanent source of industry and capital, like the stone wharves and piers of the City of New York. But new credits must ever spring up, which are the incipient condition of new improvements, public and private, and all fixed forms of capital. There must always be expansion enough in the currency to set all the capacity for useful labor in the country to work. This is the only limit to the expansion of credits. Gold and silver ceased long ago in the history of the world to serve as an adequate representative of all those exchanges which are going on in the civilized world, and which it is the proper function of money to represent. Coin has long called to its assistance "paper of credit," both private and public, not merely to represent coin as money, but to represent other real property, and ESPECIALLY THE CURRENT DAILY LABOR OF THE WORLD'S INDUSTRIAL CLASSES, whose aggregate wages any day could not be paid BY ALL THE COIN IN THE WORLD. France uses gold, silver, and paper, all as legal tenders, and keeps them all busy to satisfy her industrial and financial wants. But France could not get along a single day with the coin alone which is within its borders, or with paper that merely represented coin as currency. This being the fact, as every one ought to know who talks on this subject, it is a most preposterous claim that coin alone can serve as legal tender, or paper always convertible into coin. You may adopt the legal fiction that all legal tenders should be convertible into coin at the will of the holder, but you cannot carry out this in fact; and the failure to carry it out at any given time, for any cause, may produce a "panic," with all its disasters.

REP.—But what would you have the Government do in reference to its present policy?

MR. C.—The course is plain. Let the Government issue, not only all the legal tenders, but all that passes in the shape of money—all should have the "image and superscription" of the Government, whether it be coin or paper. Let the Government start from a fact, that there has been, and is now, through its instrumentality and necessities, so many millions of legal tenders and bank paper or currency set afloat, which, with the Government bonds now out, represent so much credit resting on the honor and ability of the Government to pay, but furnishing also the basis for a great amount of credit in the financial system of the country. On this the country has been depending, and with this it has been at work, in all its industries and trade, since the credit paper came into existence.

The Government has no right to take away these tools, that have set so much work on foot, from the people. IT IS NOT JUSTICE. Suppose a man has engaged another in the enterprise of building a house or factory, by promising to furnish all the tools, and by giving a certain valuation or rent for it when it is finished. Then at a certain stage of the process of erection, the proprietor takes away a part of the tools necessary to finish the work, and, moreover, diminishes the valuation of both work and material. Would not that be considered a great act of injustice, especially if the builder had no remedy in law against the proprietor? Now, this is precisely what the Government has done to the industrial part of the nation, with the additional injustice of COMPULSION in its dealings with the people who are not the moneyed and the governing class. The Government, during a time of great exigency, issued millions of credit paper, on the strength of which the people willingly furnished labor and material to carry on a war of self-preservation against rebellion and disruption. But not only that, the people began to build up the country on the strength of this same credit paper; they set on foot new enterprises, built railroads, factories, and opened new mines and farms on the same credit, and by the facilities for paying labor and material which this Government currency afforded. After the war was over the Government began to contract this currency, and to tax the people, in order to buy its bonds before they were yet due; which policy contracted credit so much the more; and it has continued to pursue systematically a policy of contraction, for the purpose, as alleged, to resume specie payments on this currency. The people do not want specie; they want the CREDITS already given them NOT TO BE WITHDRAWN; they want their labor and material freely given to save the country, or to build it up, to be valued by the same standard as that by which it was measured when they began to work. The moneyed class obviously want scarce money and high rates of interest. This gives them more power and less expense. But the advantage of the whole people, including this very moneyed class, if their interests were rightly understood, is to have credit easy to the industrious, the honest, and the enterprising, and the interest of money more nearly equitable.

REP.—What, then, Mr. Cooper, would be your specific remedy for the financial troubles which involve the country at present? What would be the policy you would recommend for the action of Congress?

MR. C.—At present Congress has devised no better plan for the financial policy of the country than this. Congress has passed a law that specie payments for all currency shall be resumed in 1879, and to provide for this it has authorized the Treasurer of the United States to withdraw currency until the present volume shall shrink from four hundred to three hundred millions; and he is further authorized to sell bonds at 4 or 4½ per cent. interest, to the amount necessary to get the specie wherewith to resume payments. As the 5 per cent. bonds, outstanding, are only at par now, I think the prospect is very poor for selling the 4 or 4½ per cent. without ruinous discounts and large addition to the debt of the nation. If the banks also are made to do business and issue their notes only on a specie basis, instead of bonds as now, it will shrink their currency so as to bring another panic.

But if the banks are allowed to give credits secured by Government bonds, why should not the Government itself do the same? If it will hurt the banks, and cripple and curtail so much their resources for giving credit, why is not such a policy objectionable as to the credits given by the Government? But here is precisely the point of departure of the moneyed class from the people at large. They wish to monopolize not only *private* but all *public* credits. All credits under the sanction and provision of law and the Government ought to be *public* credits, for which the Government alone should be held responsible. Such is any paper currency now, even if it is not legal tender. Nothing but a legal sanction can pass a bank-note into the circulation of the country. The credit of the bank is indorsed by the Government, in order to be regarded as good. The Government, under the present system, often borrows its own indorsement! But the first point of departure I would have from this whole system of finance is, that everything, gold, silver, or paper, that passes into the circulation of the country as money should have the Government's "image and superscription" upon it, and should be issued and controlled entirely by the Government, so that there shall be no legalized money, directly or indirectly, belonging to private corporations. This is a part of that "special and class legislation" that I have always contended against as the bane of republican institutions.

Now, I would have Congress repeal this last act of contraction of the people's credits in the shape of currency, while it is an expansion of credits to the moneyed class, in the shape of bonds.

I would have Congress pass an act that should make all currency that of the Government alone; and, of course, I should abolish the present bank currency, giving these institutions the option of doing business only on legal tenders; these they may secure at any time, by simply giving up to the Government an equivalent amount of Government bonds, whose interest thereafter stops until bought up again by legal tenders. This will extinguish the interest-bearing debt of the country in part, by one not bearing interest.

Secondly, to start all fairly and justly, I would have Congress pass an act restoring the currency in volume to the condition in which it was at the close of the war, or soon after; when, peace being declared, the whole nation sprang to the arts of peace with the energy of war; when they took these very credits, which the necessities of Government had furnished, as the price of the nation's life, and began to build up the country still more securely in the wealth and products of "myriad-handed industry;" when their hopes and their faith were stimulated to new life by this mighty credit poured into the circulation of the country, and all the property of the country and its products were measured and exchanged by the new standard; when none were found idle except the shiftless and those who sought idleness; when no factory stopped its production for want of consumers, for all were consumers, because all were producers. I would have all that currency restored to the country, and not withdrawn or contracted by taxing the property of the country to pay it; but allowed to remain, till it had produced its equivalent by the industry and products which it brought into existence.

I would have this whole volume of currency made as permanent and invariable a measure of property and exchange as possible, by neither increasing nor diminishing its volume by any arbitrary law; but rather use the agency of Government to keep at its present stated volume, by issuing it again with one hand for labor, service, and bonds, while it received it with the other as currency. I would have this specific volume of the currency from which we shall now start, henceforth and forever, never diminished at all, and only increased as per capita, very gradually and imperceptibly, as statistics shall show, and a rule of increase founded thereon, as the exchanges and the population of the country increase. And this would be virtually equivalent to making the currency a permanent and unfluctuating standard of values; for it would keep it in the same ratio or relative measure to all the property of the country and the increase of its population. I would thus make the stated volume of currency which has been forced upon the country at one time, but which now threatens the most unhappy consequences if it be withdrawn—I would make this one volume an unvarying measure for all time, by giving it an expansion by rule and statistical measure of slow application, and such as would never derange prices or permit fluctuations. I would not increase the bonded debt of the country either, except by rule and statistical measure; but I would change its form from the present high rate of interest, and from so large a portion payable in gold to foreigners, into a debt of equitable rate of interest, and payable to our own citizens.

Rep.—But how can this be done without repudiation and dishonor to the country?

Mr. C.—No vested rights can stand in the face of the public welfare; common and statute law recognizes this principle. Hence, all vested rights can be repealed by the law-making power that conferred them. Under this principle, private property can be taken for public use, and all corporate rights can be abolished that stand in the way of the public welfare—but never without proper compensation to the parties that may be losers; and of this, the public administration must appoint the means and provide the regulations. But I propose to change the character of the bonded debt by a voluntary process.

First. Whoever needs currency must give up the Government bonds for it. The compulsion here is in making every one do business and pay debts in legal tenders; and the principle for their use exclusively is that the public welfare admits of no other money.

Secondly. Whoever desires to fund the currency shall receive bonds at a lower rate of interest than that which legitimate business now gives, but which is higher than the average yearly increase of the whole property of the country. This I would fix upon as the interest of the bonds; it is now about three per cent.

There is an element of compulsion here; but as the whole country pays the interest on the public debt, it seems but just that only that amount of interest should be paid, which the increase in the public wealth justifies, and no more.

Rep.—But how will you prevent the too rapid funding of the currency, and keep it at a steady volume, as you propose?

Mr. C.—This "too rapid funding" is, I think, a groundless fear, considering the low rate of interest given. Because, in a country like this, so active, so enterprising, and so full of new resources, the opportunities and the solicitation for safe investments is far greater than in the old country, and would naturally tend to draw money from funding; so that the calls for currency would be equal, if not superior, to the applications for funding. But as the Government controls the whole matter, it can keep an "*even hand*" by allowing neither the funded debt nor the currency to increase beyond a certain ratio to each other. As the currency was received it might be paid out again for service, material, or bonds; as the bonds were received they could be paid out again for service, material, or currency. Thus the whole of the circulation between bonds and currency could be kept even.

This great bonded debt of the country would really become the refuge and security of the widow and the fatherless, and those poor and ignorant people who cannot invest their little savings in legitimate business, even through others, because they cannot trust them, and have no ability to watch the safety or protect the use and return of their money. The public debt would become the poor man's "savings bank," instead of being, as now, the exchequer of the rich, and the means of pampering wealth and idleness. Benevolent institutions, churches, and college endowments would seek it, for the same reason, because of its *perfect safety;* and even the same funded interests of Europe would seek investment in this country for security, and will gladly pay gold for all the bonds they could buy, at a little higher interest than their own countries could afford.

Rep.—But what about the *gold* all this time, which is now very much mixed up with this question of finance, because it is so universally the legal tender of civilized nations?

Mr. C.—It might be a part of our legal tender still. France makes gold, silver, and paper all legal tenders; why cannot we? But if any one wants gold as a *commodity*, let him buy it as any other commodity, at the market price. Let such exchange currency or any other commodity for gold, as suits their convenience and the state of the market, which no government can control without tyranny and interference with private rights. That whole subject will take care of itself, and the whole circulation of the world will naturally mingle and interchange with our national circulation, as the outer air mingles and interchanges with the air of the room, if passages are left free.

Rep.—I understand you, then, Mr. Cooper, that you regard this whole contest about the currency as a conflict between the "vested rights" of the whole moneyed class and their interests, "but ill understood," and the rights and interests of the whole people; that you regard the whole legislation of Congress on this subject, with little exception, as made in the interests of class, special, and partial legislation, which has been, thus far, the bane of our republican institutions; because, under forms of law, it sacrifices the people to classes of special privileges; and I understand your present remedy for all the present evils and all the future that are likely to occur from our system of finance, is, that Government alone issue all currency and whatever circulates as money, and makes this currency *interconvertible* with bonds, which the Government can control, and not with gold, which it cannot control; and further that the Government start in the present emergency, from precisely that volume of credits in currency and in bonds, that was set afloat by the irresistible necessities of the war for the Union; that this volume should be sustained substantially as it was soon after the close of the war, when it rose to its maximum; and be made the measure of all values, and the means of exchanges for all coming time—subject only to the slow increase of volume which statistics shall justify as the increase of population, and its ratio, per capita, to the currency.

Mr. C.—That is precisely what I propose; and my efforts to bring this subject before the public are heartily seconded by many able gentlemen.

Rep.—But it appears to me, Mr. Cooper, you place great power in the hands of the Government by such a policy. It may lead to enormous speculations and peculations on the part of individuals and officials. Politics will become a trade more than ever, because of their close connection with finance, commerce, and moneyed institutions. Some administration may ride again and again into power, and overthrow finally all the free institutions of the country with a great flood of currency, which it can manufacture in unlimited quantities by a slight change in the laws that Congress may be induced to enact at any time.

Mr. C.—It would require almost a treatise on republican government to answer all your objections, and then you could not be answered if you had no faith in free principles and democratic forms, and in the paternal functions of a government instituted " by the people and for the people." The slave-holders of our country had to learn this lesson at last, and I do not know any vested rights in property so enormous, or so intelligent and well organized resistance as slavery brought to bear upon the free institutions of this country. And yet the slave-holding portion of this country will find itself the greatest gainer by its losses. They lost in the conflict, chiefly through the might of *truth* and justice, which will be their great gain. We shall have many conflicts, doubtless, between the people on one side, and moneyed, social, or religious classes organized with certain claims, and even vested rights; but never again so great a conflict as the slave-holders brought about. I think the Union and the Republic may be regarded as safe for a long time to come. The people can and will control this Government in their own interests in the future, as well as in the past, precisely in proportion as they can be made conscious of their power and their rights. The forms of the Constitution and laws are all favorable to them now, but their understanding is darkened by bad counsels. The Government is already, and ought to be in a still larger measure, *paternal*. It should aim constantly to " establish justice," and organize love and right into law. If we can teach the people justice and truth, they will see to it that the " Republic suffers no detriment." There is nothing that I can perceive in the policy I advise that will place any uncontrollable power in the hands of any Administration or Congress. If the law will not protect the people's rights, let provisions of the Constitution be resorted to. Let us have a " civil service " that will make office under Government more of a " professional " and regular occupation than of trade and bargain for place and patronage. Let the

United States embody in their Constitution, as has the State of New York, that there shall be "no special, *partial*, or *class legislation*," and make its laws on the currency conform to this provision of the Constitution.

The question of the currency is of boundless importance to the American people. The stability of our Government will depend on a wise settlement of this momentous interest.

The American people will never allow this subject to rest until it is safely moored to that sure foundation of the eternal principles of truth and justice on which our fathers placed the Constitution of these United States.

Our fathers meant that the Government should be of the people and for the people. They intended to embody the "wisdom of simplicity" into law, and make it a shield of protection for the unsuspecting masses of the people against those that are resorting to all forms of art to obtain property without labor. The framers of the Constitution would never have recommended one kind of money for the issues of the Government, and another for the people.

Under the circumstances in which our Government was placed at the close of the late war, they would have taken the advice of their most venerated member, Benjamin Franklin, who said that "paper money, well-founded, has great advantages over gold and silver, being light, and convenient for handling in large sums, and not likely to be reduced by demand for exportation."

"On the whole," he says, "no method has hitherto been found to establish a medium of trade, equal in all its advantages to bills of credit made a general legal tender."

If I have done, or can do anything to restore the tools of trade to the American people, to enable them to work out the salvation of our country from the present paralyzed condition of trade and commerce, I shall regard it as a treasure that "moth and rust cannot corrupt,"— one that will brighten while life and thought and immortality endures.

AN OPEN LETTER

TO PRESIDENT R. B. HAYES.

By Peter Cooper.

New York, August 6, 1877.

Although I have but lately addressed you an open letter on the sad state of the industrial and financial conditions of our common country, and the causes that have brought it about, yet the events that have since transpired, while they have given additional emphasis to that appeal, justify me in once more addressing you on the same subject.

Surely the peaceful expostulations and complaints of so many thousands of your fellow-citizens, going up from every part of this distressed country, not to speak of the violence and lawlessness which this distress has occasioned, not only appeal to your humanity and patriotism, but call for the most earnest and instant action on the part of the Government of which you are the chief Executive.

From your past patriotic life and action, and from your present wise and conciliating conduct in the political affairs of this country, we have every reason to hope a new and straight path of relief will be found for the manifest evils under which this country is laboring.

It is with this hope, and, at my advanced age, with no other motive than the welfare of our beloved country, that I unite with thousands of my fellow-citizens in calling your attention, and that of your political advisers, not only to the facts, which are obvious enough, but to the causes and the remedies that ought to be considered in devising the best means of curing the present evils. The facts themselves are appalling to any patriotic heart.

More than two hundred thousand men, within the last few weeks, have joined in "strikes" on the various railroad lines, the workshops, and the mines of the country, on account of further reduction in their wages, already reduced to the living point. That some of these strikes have been attended with lawless and unjustifiable violence, only shows the intensity of the evils complained of, and the despair of the sufferers. For four years past, since the "panic of 1873," millions of men and women, in this hitherto rich and prosperous country, have been thrown out of employment, or living on precarious and inadequate wages, have felt embittered with a lot in which neither economy nor industry, nor a cheerful willingness to work hard, can bring any alleviation.

Is it to be wondered at that *enforced idleness* has made tramps of so

7

many of our laboring population, or induced them to join the criminal and dangerous classes?

During this same period, immigration into this country of the hardy and industrious of all nations, who have hitherto built up our country, has, in a great measure, stopped, while thousands of artisans and mechanics whom a prosperous country cannot spare, are emigrating to other countries. Our manufactories are, many of them, closed, or running at a loss, or giving starvation prices to their operatives. Our merchants are demanding the reduction of their rents, discharging many of their employés, and such as are in debt are fast going into bankruptcy. The mining and railroad interests of the country, on which the income and the employment of so many thousands depend, are fast succumbing to the general failure in the finances of the country, so that their stocks have become depreciated or worthless, and their employés discharged or mutinous on account of reduced wages. Real estate has depreciated to less than half of what it would have brought four years ago ; much of it cannot be sold for any price, and mortgages of one-quarter its value, if foreclosed, swallow up the whole. The thriving and enterprising farmer of the West, especially, feels this rise in the value of money, as compared with labor or property. With the hardy toil of years, he has opened and improved his farm, and the comparative small loan, which laid but a light weight on the resources of his land in prosperous times, and with a sufficiency money, is now threatening to swallow up the labor of his life ! Even the banks and the loaning institutions, not being able to invest their money on " good securities," are embarrassed on both sides—the failure of their debtors, that throws so many of the securities on their hands, and makes " bonds and mortgages " a " glut in the market," and the difficulty of making any new loans or investments—so that money " goes a begging " at one and a half and two per cent. !

But these moneyed men are very patient with their troubles in this respect, for they know that *money is appreciating in value all the time!* It may be now that loanable capital, on good security, is gathered largely in the moneyed centres, and much of it comparatively idle ; but this is no great hardship to those that own the capital, in the presence of the fact, that money is *appreciating* in its relative value while waiting for active investment. This is the secret why money seeks no active investment now, but only good security, or idleness. The country at large, its various industrial enterprises, and its labor, *are in want of money*. Is there any fact more obvious than this? Nor is it the rich that want money, but the poor, as a necessary condition for selling the labor which is their sole possession. Hence, to the poor man, *cheap money is equivalent to cheap bread.*

Ever since 1865, this country has been *losing its* money.

During the last ten years, thousands of millions of money have been swallowed in Government and railroad bonds and other securities, and in importations which, till lately, have far exceeded our exportations. It is a fact on record in the books of the United States Treasury, and by such authorities as Spaulding in his " History of the Currency," Mr. Maynard, Chairman of the Committee on Banking and Currency in Congress, and Spinner, Assistant-Secretary of the Treasury, that this country had, up to the year 1865, issued in different forms of currency and treasury notes, current as money among the people, $2,192,395,527 ! This vast sum had, on the first of November, 1873, shrunk to $631,-488,676 (see *Congressional Record*, March 31, 1874).

In the year 1865 there was in the hands of the people, as a currency, $58 per head ; in 1875 the currency of all kinds was only a little more than $17 per head.

You may call this currency a vast debt of the people, as it was incurred by the Government to save the life of the nation. But it was *money—every dollar of it.* It was paid by the Government "for value received ; " it was used by the people to pay their debts, to measure the value of their property, and, as your present Secretary of the Treasury said in his seat in the Senate, "every citizen of the United States had conformed his business to the legal tender clause."

This currency was also the creature of law, and under the entire control of the Government, but held in trust for the benefit of the people, as are all its functions. Was it either just or humane to allow $1,100,000,000 of this currency, a large part bearing no interest, but paying labor, and fructifying every business enterprise, to be absorbed into bonds in the space of eight years, bearing a heavy interest, of which the bondholder bore no share? (See Spaulding's "History of the Currency.") The Government seemed to administer this vast currency as if there were but one interest in the nation to be promoted, and that the profit of those who desired to fund their money with the *greatest security,* and to make money scarce and of high rate of interest! *This is the issue of the hour ; this is the battle of the people, and for the people, in which the present administration is called upon to declare which side it will take.* If this policy was unjust and ruinous at the first, it is unjust and ruinous now. If it has led us from prosperity into adversity, the only course is *to retrace our steps,* to stop this funding any longer, and give the people back their money, justly earned, and hardly won by the toils, perils, and sacrifices of the people. But as this vast and life-giving currency has now gone irretrievably into bonds, and the bonds have gone largely abroad for importations, that have still further depressed the industry of our people by buying abroad what we could and should have manufactured at home, I would respectfully suggest the following policy for your administration in the present emergency and for the future prosperity of the people of this country :

' *First.* Let the Government give immediate relief to unemployed labor, either through definite methods of help, given to settlers of unoccupied lands in the West, or by great and obvious public improvements which are seen to be necessary to the prosperity and safety of the country—such as a North-western and a South-western Railroad. Both these methods might be used, in view of the great distress, now, of the laboring classes. The railroads will invite settlements, protect the country from Indian wars, more costly than the railroads themselves, and give employment and the money which will enable the poor man to settle the lands. Even State and municipal help might be evoked to this end of employing labor, by issuing currency, for the bonds of States and Municipalities that could employ labor profitably in any local improvements.

Secondly. Restore the silver coinage as a legal tender ; and while it swells the currency, it may be made as light as paper, for transportation, by "Bills of Exchange," or by a currency that represents silver. The demonetization of silver was a trick of the enemies of the poor man's currency. The remonetization of silver will be a great relief now, in the depression of all business, if not the final and best measure.

Thirdly. Let us adopt a permanent policy of public finance that shall hereafter control both the volume and the value of the national currency, in the interest of the whole people, and not of a class. Let us have a national currency fully honored by the Government, and not as now, partially demonetized—the sole currency and legal tender of the country, taken for all duties and taxes, and interconvertible with the bonds, at a low but equitable rate of interest. This will forever take the creation of currency, and its extinction, out of the hands of banks and those interested in making it scarce and high, and put it completely under the control of law and the interests of the people.

Fourthly. Let us promote and instruct industry, all over the land, by founding, under National, State and municipal encouragement, INDUSTRIAL SCHOOLS of every kind that can advance *skill in labor.* The rich need the literary and professional school and colleges, and they should have them ; but the poor need the *industrial school of art and science ;* and it should be made the duty of the local governments to provide a practical education for the mass of the people, as the best method of "guaranteeing to every State a republican form of government."

Fifthly. The Government can do much towards promoting the industry of this people, and encouraging capital to enter upon works of manufacture, by a judicious tariff upon all importations of which we have the raw material in abundance, and the labor ready to be employed in the production. It is no answer to this to say, "Buy where you can cheapest." I have said before, "We cannot, as a nation, buy anything cheap that leaves our own good raw materials unused, and our own labor unemployed."

Sixthly. Let us have a civil service as well organized and specific as the military or naval service. Let us take the civil service out of mere political partisanship, and put such appointments upon the ground of honesty, capacity, and educational fitness, so that no man can hold his office and receive its emoluments without a faithful discharge of the duties prescribed by the law. The noble and efficient recognition that you have already given to this principle, in divorcing politics from the ordinary clerical and civil service of the country, entitles you to the thanks of every citizen.

By these methods of immediate relief and future administration, we may pass safely, I think, the great crisis through which our beloved country is now laboring.

"The producing cause of all prosperity," says Daniel Webster, "is labor, labor, labor." * * *

"The Government was made to protect this industry—to give it both encouragement and security. To this very end, with this precise object in view, power was given to Congress over the currency, and over the money of the country."

Though the influences that are now working against the rights of labor and the true interests of a republican government, are insidious and concealed under plausible reasons, yet the danger to our free institutions now, is no less than in the inception of the rebellion that shook our republic to its centre. It is only another oligarchy, another enslaving power that is asserting itself against the interest of the whole people. There is, fast forming in this country, an aristocracy of wealth—the worst form of aristocracy that can curse the prosperity of any country. For such an aristocracy *has no country*—" absenteeism," living abroad, while they draw their income from the country, is one of its common characteristics. Such an aristocracy is without soul and without patriotism. Let us save our country from this, its most potent, and, as I hope, its last enemy. Let your fellow-citizens beseech you, Mr. President, to consider well what the crisis of the country demands of you and your political advisers, not losing sight of the fact that there are great wrongs that must be righted in the administration of the finances of this country for the last twelve years. Old issues of North and South are, in a great measure, passing away, and that patriotism and far-sightedness that has so far guided your administration, we hope and trust, will find a way to relieve the present distress of the country. There is no section of our common country that needs so much the reviving influence of an abundant and a sound currency, as the South. The Southern people have the finest natural resources that our country affords; every facility for manufacture—the material, labor, and water-power indefinite. They need only money, wisely distributed among its working and enterprising population; and it was well said, lately, by one of the Southern statesmen, that the "*Government had impoverished, discomfited, and crushed the South more by its financial policy, since peace was declared, than by its arms during the whole war of rebellion*"!

If the people can look for no relief from the present Congress and Administration—if those who now sway the financial interests of the country cannot see their great opportunity—then *new men* must be chosen by the people whom they can trust to make laws, and execute measures that " shall secure the blessings of liberty to themselves and their posterity."